D1462022

ANOTHER WORLD

ANOTHER WORLD

An autobiographical novel by

JAN MYRDAL

Translated by
Alan Bernstein

RAVENSWOOD BOOKS • CHICAGO

ISTKW

Originally published in Sweden as En Annan Värld
by P.A. Norstedt & Söners Förlag, Stockholm, 1984.
English translation published in 1994.
Printed in the United States of America

Library of Congresss Cataloging-in-Publication Data

Myrdal, Jan
[Annan värld. English]
Another World / Jan Myrdal : translated by Alan
Bernstein.
ISBN 1-884468-00-4
1. Myrdal, Jan — Childhood and youth.
2. Authors, Swedish—20th century—Biography.
I.   Title.
PT9876.23.Y7Z46313   1994
839.7'837403—dc20
[B]   93-41239
                                             CIP

ANOTHER WORLD

CHAPTER 1

The picture from autumn 1938 is perfectly distinct. I am lying on the sofa, momentarily looking up from my book. I am wearing short pants, my hair has been recently cut, and I am lying on my stomach with my head raised, gazing left. I look aft, through the open door on the starboard side and across the landing, to where the ship's gift shop is still closed. There are no people around. In the background, the silver meanders of the frieze shine above the doorway leading into the Cabin Class salon.

I feel the shudder of the engines and I am rocked by the slow heaving of the ship. Silence surrounds me and I am alone. Shifting my gaze, I see a globe on the jacaranda bookshelf. The armchairs are covered in brown leather. The tables in front of me are inlaid with silver. There are magazines on them, stacked neatly. It has all been recently tidied up. The bright covers of the magazines shine against the dark tables. I can see the spine of the large atlas—strong, broad binding and gold tooling. The walls are covered in light pigskin and the ceiling is of gray walnut. It is September 1938 and I am eleven years old. Eleven years, one month and sixteen days.

It was still early morning. I was all alone here in the Cabin Class library. All the doors stood open and everything was newly cleaned. There were no passengers and no crew about, and I could smell leather, the sea, floor polish and something that might have been cigar smoke from the corridor. I turned back to my book and went on reading *One Thousand and One Nights*. I had taken the first of the six volumes from the shelf yesterday afternoon. I was now well into the second volume. Sinbad was down in the hole surrounded by corpses. The rock blocking the opening had just been removed, and the sudden flash of light stung the

eyes, as they lowered a dead man along with his young and still
living wife down into the pit. She cried and moaned. I seized a
large bone from one of the skeletons lying around and then killed
her with it. I took the food she had brought along with her and I
took her jewels. It now dawned on me that I would survive, even
here, on my fourth voyage.

And that is why I had stopped reading, looked off through the
empty rooms, listened to the far-off engines and felt the rolling of
the ship. Had it really been necessary to kill her? There was a
footnote at the bottom of the page, written by the professor who
had translated the book from Arabic. It was the kind of thing that
might have been written by Miss Rehn of Ålsten School, which I
had put behind me forever. It said that one should pay no attention to this, as it was a peculiarly Oriental way of behaving, and
that Westerners thought in a different way. But I didn't believe it.
That wasn't the reason I had looked up. The woman lowered into
the pit had had food with her, and yet, everyone let down into the
hole was destined to die. In this land the living accompanied the
dead. The food was just meant to tide them over on the short
journey. They would all die. There lay thousands of old corpses
around me. I had already noticed this as they were lowering me
down, and I shouted and begged them up there to spare my life. I
looked towards the light and saw the heads of my good neighbors, friends, relatives and in-laws outlined against the blue sky.
They all stared down at me as they slowly lowered me into the
hole. I wasn't able to see their expressions, because their faces
were hidden in shadow. I only saw a wreath of heads around the
opening and it looked as if the eyes were flashing in the shadowy
faces of my friends and relatives. I clung to the rope as my family
slowly let me down, and in the light from the opening, I saw all
the dead bodies beneath me. They lay as though on display down
there. But in the corners of the cavern, where the light grew dim,
the bodies seemed as though they had been torn apart. Yes, the

decaying remains there were spread around as if big animals had been tearing at them. I tried to hold onto the rope tightly, to be pulled back up and saved, but my neighbors and in-laws only yanked hard at the rope, testing it a little, and then a second time, pulling all together with a violent jerk, so that my fingers lost their grip and I fell backwards against the body of my dead wife. Then I saw the rope slowly disappear up towards the blue circle of sky, the rock fell back into place with a crash, and darkness engulfed me.

Next, as I groped around in the darkness, I stumbled over corpses everywhere. Some of them were already totally decayed; what had once been a skull turned to dust in my hand. The pit was a place of burial. Anyone who came down here could abandon all hope. I had been buried alive among all the dead. I, too, will soon be dead, I told myself, as the rock was placed over the opening. It stank here. It must have taken me a long time to get used to the stench, but I did. At the same time, I noticed that my meager supply of food was running out. I shook the water jug, but couldn't hear any water inside. I was doomed to die of thirst before I starved to death. Just then, the rock was rolled away again and the woman was sent down with her dead husband. With her, the funeral entourage had sent a jug of water and a packet of food. So it wasn't strange that I groped for a heavy bone when I saw the stone slowly roll away and then hid myself in the shadow at the edge of the light while she was lowered down. As the stone fell into place again I took advantage of the last light to smash her skull with one well-aimed blow to the head and killed her. It was either her life or mine and it's better for one to survive than for both to die. The professor hadn't understood that and Miss Rehn didn't understand such things, and that was why he wrote the footnote.

But I know that I had looked up from my book towards the landing and salon because I was thinking about something entirely different. There was another picture that had surfaced, as the dead man's young widow was lowered down towards me in tears. I had looked up from the book to make sure that I was alone and that no one could see me as I saw it. It was a picture further on in the book, where the villainous Christian bandit Barsum carried off the slave Emerald. She twisted about, lifting her arms and leaving her clothing in disarray. You could see her breasts and the hair in her armpits as she called on God for help. And now, as the dead man's young widow was let down, she had long black hair that streamed in the wind and her thin dress was in disarray and I looked at her. Actually, it wasn't necessary to kill her. Now that she was in the pit, you could have fucked her. Maybe several people would die up there this week, and you could kill their husbands and wives and take their food instead. Or something.

And I saw all of this suddenly in strongly colored images right in front of the page, and although I knew I was all alone I looked up from the book to see if anyone was there who could see what I was thinking. But I was alone in the library, alone on the entire deck, as far as I could see. Now I could have pursued this line of thought and taken out more pictures, but this really wasn't what I wanted to think about; it was light and morning, and somebody might come along any time. Instead, I looked carefully at the silver meander shining from the polished black frieze on the landing, at the globe and the silver inlay of the tables. And I listened to the great engines, felt the heaving of the ship, looked back down at my book and went on reading and killing widows and widowers, collecting gold and jewels, until the time came when the wild animals showed me the way out of the pit and I came to the green ocean that roared below.

No other Cabin Class passengers were up yet. They were still lolling around in their cabins. It was early Sunday morning, September 4, 1938, and we were out on the North Atlantic. The MS *Kungsholm* was not yet halfway to New York. This was her seventy-first voyage west, according to the passenger list. The ship was not fully booked. There were 441 empty berths, mostly in Tourist Class, our steward had told me when I had asked.

The whole family was on its way to America. All the newspapers had reported that Professor Myrdal was going to America. Gunnar was to direct a major research project, aimed at solving the "Negro Problem." He was to have many assistants and a large staff. The Carnegie Foundation in America was paying for it. We were quite an entourage as we boarded the ship in Gothenburg. We looked like something straight out of the newsreels. First came the hand luggage. Then came my parents. They carried large bouquets given them in farewell. They turned, smiled and waved, as if they were looking into a camera. Gunnar wore a gray felt hat, American style. He was not wearing an overcoat, but a single-breasted American suit he had bought in Boston on a visit there earlier that summer. Alva was dressed more in the French style. Her coat had wide lapels and large shoulder pads. Her hair shone; it was newly curled and tinted. Then came my two sisters. They were dressed up in traveling clothes. They were dressed alike, with black, school-girl hats fastened with black bows under their chins, yellow coats, white knee socks and white shoes. They wore pink silk ribbons in their hair. Behind, the better to keep an eye on them, came the governess and the newly hired young house-keeper, who was from Gothenburg. She seemed nice, although I hadn't had time to talk with her yet. I brought up the rear. I had been dressed in new, dark blue shorts, with a wide Boy Scout belt (although I was a Young Eagle) a white shirt, which had already lost its top button, a horizontally striped tie, white knee socks (which sagged), new brown shoes, a herringbone overcoat and matching cap. I looked off to the side and dragged my feet a bit, as I walked there behind them, trying to look as though I wasn't with them. I pretended that it was just a coincidence I was walking in the same direction as the others. As if I were someone else, traveling with different people, on some business of my own. But I made sure I didn't fall so far behind that Alva would ask Gunnar to turn around and call to me to catch up, so that everyone would look at me.

Mary had stayed in Sweden. She hadn't wanted to go with the family to America. We were all traveling Cabin Class. I had my own cabin with bathroom on the port side of A-deck. It was right across from the barbershop.

I don't remember if I had eaten breakfast that morning. I must have, since I wasn't hungry. If I had, it must have been half a grapefruit, followed by a bowl of shredded wheat with sliced bananas and milk. The menu read: *Shredded Wheat with Sliced Bananas and Milk.* I know this is what I had begun to eat now that I was on my way to America. But the dining room wasn't open yet. It was just after seven, and the library and salons had recently been unlocked. So I really don't know if I had eaten. I don't think so. All I remember of that morning of September 4, 1938, are those moments in the library and the fact that I woke up early in my cabin.

We were heading west, so the nights were longer and the clocks were moved forward while we slept. I woke up and lay a moment with my eyes closed, feeling the action of the far-off engines. The ship was enormous. It was like being inside a huge animal, whose heart beat slow and steady.

After waking, I lay there unmoving, not really wanting to be wide awake. Instead, I tried to see the engines in my mind, but nothing distinct appeared. So I put it into words and said:

"Two main engines of 18,000 horsepower. Double-acting cylinders and three diesel generators."

As I said this, I could see the enormous engines there in the cabin with me. The steel was blue, the copper flamed red and the brass gleamed. But I can't remember if I had been down in the engine room yet, or had actually seen the engines.

My bed was a bunk. I had a reading lamp on the wall above my head. It was like the sleeping car on the night train from Stockholm to Gothenburg, when I had traveled second class for the first time. But this was better and fancier still. The bunk was wider and more comfortable than the one on the train, and there was a newly-polished brass railing around this one. Not at the foot of the bed, of course; you had to be able to get down without climbing over it. The brass railing was there so the passengers wouldn't be thrown to the floor if the ship began to roll. But she never rolled. She was equipped with anti-rolling tanks, and just heaved along on the heavy swells. Slowly she rocked, and you could feel her move beneath your feet as you walked the decks. The whole time you could hear a low, creaking sound coming from inside the engines. The storms had not yet begun for the year. I got out of my bunk and the carpet felt soft and pleasant beneath my feet. Walking on it was like going down a warm summer road, where the gravel had been ground into gray dust, and the pile of the carpet felt soft between my toes like old horse droppings. The kind that have reached the point where they are nice and dry under the feet. I had got up on my knees on the sofa and pulled open the curtains. The window facing the port side promenade was not a real window but a porthole, just as there were decks and not floors on board. But it wasn't round like a regular steamship porthole, the kind I saw when I used to take the boat on Lake Mälaren from Stockholm to Stallarholmen to visit my paternal grandfather. No, this one was rectangular, like a window on land. My cabin was located astern, where the promenade was not glassed in. There were still no Tourist Class passengers out on their A-deck promenade, but it was already light and the sea was green and I could see that it was windy. Here inside, where it was quiet, I could hear only the far-off engines, I thought about how the great waves sputtered as the foam swirled past all white and fresh, leaving a taste of salt in the mouth when you stood out there on deck.

The sky was cloudless, as clear as glass. It was a light bottle green, I thought. As if I were standing in a cabin behind a tinfoil porthole on a model ship in a bottle on someone's mantlepiece. Uncle Folke made me a ship in a bottle last summer, but it wasn't an ocean liner. It was a fishing boat and it had taken a lot of intricate work to raise the mast and paint the plaster of Paris ocean, once he got the boat inside. It looked great when the mast was raised, the plaster painted, the bottle corked and sealed with red sealing wax. When they saw the ship in the bottle, people must have wondered how it got in there. I left it in the workshop at Kvicksta.

"There's no point taking the bottle to America," he said. "You can get it when you come back."

Then I saw the ocean sputter out there again. It was so beautiful there with no people on deck that you really ached with joy the way you do on mornings when everything is peaceful and no one else is up.

We had sailed from Gothenburg three days earlier. Later that first night I had been up on the promenade deck, hanging over the railing like all the others, looking out into the darkness where Sweden had been. And I imagined that when he saw his native country disappear he spoke in a voice so loud and clear that everyone was surprised. They almost recoiled in fear, raised their hands and turned to look at him as he stood sunk in dark thoughts at the railing with the storm combing his hair.

"Nevermore!"

I had also begun to study English and felt it was right to say this in English, now that I had decided never to return to Sweden. The others were only going to be in America for a couple of years. Both Alva and Gunnar had been there before, and Gunnar had already been there once this year to receive an honorary degree and take part in the Swedish-American commemoration. It was three hundred years ago that Kalmare Nyckel and Fågel Grip arrived at what is today Wilmington, Delaware, where we had bought land from the Indians and built the fort Christina Skans. But after only sixteen years the Dutch took the colony away from us, so the whole thing didn't last very long. But if the others intended to remain only a few years in America, I had different plans. I was emigrating. I was never going to go back to Europe. But I kept this decision to myself. Naturally, I said nothing out loud that the others might hear. I just thought it to myself.

I had made up my mind in the early summer. But I had been thinking about it ever since I first heard that we were going to America. I had gone to the library at the Sigtuna Foundation to read up on the New World. But the crucial decision to return to Sweden *nevermore* was made early that summer. It was while I sat talking to Träff in the kennel at Kvicksta that it really dawned on me that I was seeing him, and Kvicksta, for the last time, that I was now going away forever to start a new life in another world. I stroked Träff on the nose up towards his eyes and head, and he looked at me with his big brown eyes. I felt all hot in my chest and I almost cried. Yet, I had been thinking about it that entire spring, when I took English lessons after school. I had stood on the front platform of the Number 12 streetcar, as it carried me across the Traneberg Bridge towards the city and my English lessons, looked at the water, hills and pines, and the new apartment houses and thought that all this might belong to a former life, now that I was going away.

The first time I had told anyone of my decision was three days earlier. But there was no danger, since he didn't know who I was, and I hadn't really told him I was emigrating, but made it sound as if I was just back in the old country on a visit.

When the train had arrived in Gothenburg on Thursday morning, September 1, we had all gone to Hotel Eggers to drink coffee and eat hot cereal for breakfast. The hotel stood diagonally across from the central station. We sat on the glass-enclosed veranda. I told them I was going out to take a look at the city for awhile. I was urged to watch the time, so I wouldn't be late, miss the ship, and not get to go. I promised not to be late and went out. I walked the streets thinking that this was the last I would ever see of Sweden. And I felt no regret at the thought of leaving this country.

I stood for a moment looking down into the Great Harbor Canal. There wasn't a real railing there, just iron chains. I heard the tramcars behind me. I looked in the shop windows. The stores hadn't opened yet. Later, I looked at some cars in a showroom. I don't remember where it was. All I remember is the huge, gleaming window and the big showroom with cars inside. They were selling Fords. I stood out there in the street a long time gazing in at a blue Lincoln Zephyr, parked closest to the window. It was pretty, even if I wasn't too fond of Ford cars. Just then I saw a car salesman walk between the cars in my direction. He unlocked the door and opened for business. He let me in to take a closer look at the cars. He was in his fifties, rather fat and bald. The only hair he had was at his neck; it was gray. Tufts of red hair grew from his ears. He wore horn-rimmed glasses and a dark blue, double-breasted suit. It was the same color as the Lincoln Zephyr he had parked near the window by the street. I told him I had spent the summer with relatives in Sweden, and that now I was on my way home to America again. I was traveling by myself. At the moment, I was killing time before my ship sailed. I would be sailing on the Kungsholm to America. I told him my father was an engineer. He had been a designer for Svenska Fläktfabriken. He had lost his money in the Kreuger crash and was forced to sell our big house on Lidingö and the summer place on Dalarö and everything and emigrate. Now he worked in America for a large electrical installation company. He supervised the installation work the firm did on contract in skyscrapers. Because of this he travelled around from one coast to the other and that was how I got to see all of America. He took me along with him because my mother had died when I was just a baby. And we always stayed in hotels. I assured him that it was most practical.

While I told the car salesman this story, I looked him in the eye. The horn-rimmed glasses were very large. The right bow had been repaired. The showroom was reflected in the lenses. His eyes were tiny back there. He was near-sighted. Slowly I took a step to the left so that he was forced to turn his head, and I could see the blue Lincoln-Zephyr mirrored before his eyes. He nodded while I talked.

"Give my best to Detroit," he said later and gave me a small, blue and white enameled ashtray with raised letters inside what looked like an oil drop. They read:

Lincoln Zephyr V.12

THE STYLE LEADER.

I kept the ashtray hidden in the pocket of my overcoat when we went on board, and said nothing of my visit with the Ford salesman.

There were now some people moving in the corridor. I could hear voices out there. A man and a woman. The man growled. He spoke in a loud voice. It wasn't Standard Swedish, it was a melodious Finland-Swedish. The woman replied in monosyllable.

"Right. Right."

I looked up from *One Thousand and One Nights* and peeked out. The couple was now walking by out there in the corridor. His face was bright red. He wore checkered knickerbockers and a brown tweed jacket. His white hair was closely cropped. The woman was twenty years younger. She had short gray hair and a dark blue tailor-made suit. They must have come up out of the elevator. Now they were walking toward the veranda, called the winter garden, even though it was still summer. They had eaten breakfast. Beyond them a deck steward hurried by. He was on his way to the salon. The passengers had begun to wake up. I had set my watch when I got up and it was now nine o'clock. Still, no one came into the library; it was too early. Besides, no one travel- ing Cabin Class seemed interested in reading books. Many were interested in sports. They took long walks on deck. When the weather was good, clay pigeon shoots were arranged for them. They competed against each other. Most of their time, however, the passengers spent sitting in their deck chairs. They had rented them from the deck steward on the first day and each passenger had his own chair with his name on it. There they sat with plaid blankets around their legs. Some read, some talked, but many just slept. Others occupied themselves with various games or drank inside the bar. It was quiet in the library. I had it pretty much to myself. Now I no longer bothered to look up from my book. People were awake and I just had this corner of the library to myself. I had been found standing out on the furthest promontory of the black cliffs, waving a white shroud that I had taken from off one of the dead. The captain of the ship heading for Basra had seen me. He rescued me and took me aboard with my big bundle. In it were all the valuables I had taken from the dead people in the hole. And when I came home to Bagdad, I gave presents to widows and orphans and resumed my life of pleasure.

CHAPTER 2

The wind is blowing around me and I tell myself that the white ship, the MS Kungsholm, is plowing through the green waters of the North Atlantic. I am standing astern, on the promenade deck, leaning over the railing, in back of the lifeboats. I've been there a long time. It is already lunch time. I stand on the starboard side. If I look up from the water, and out toward the place where the sky meets the sea, the Arctic Ocean must be there beyond the horizon. We are heading West. In front of me I can see the two large funnels. They are adorned with the three golden crowns of the Swedish American Line on a blue background. But the funnels are not real ones; they are only decoration. The Kungsholm is not a steamship, she is a motor ship. We are the same age, she and I. She is made of steel. They began to build her in March 1927 at Blohm and Voss in Hamburg, and she was launched the following year. She weighs in at 20,000 gross register tons and her engines were built by Burmeister and Wain in Copenhagen. She was black at first, but now she's been painted white all over.

She is Sweden's largest ocean liner, but in fact, she is only slightly larger then Engineer Brunel's Great Eastern of 1858. And compared to the really enormous Atlantic giants I have read about, the Swedish American Line's flagship is a pretty small boat. The MS *Queen Mary* of the Cunard White Star Line is over 80,000 tons, and the French *Normandie* is even larger. but the MS *Kungsholm* is a beautiful ship and *the machinery has a sweet sound,* I tell myself in English.

If I hold my mouth open, it soon fills with a taste of salt. I am bare-headed and feel the wind on my forehead. It's not cold, just cool. The wind is rising, I tell myself. But actually, it isn't. I just tell myself that the waves are growing out there, whipped up in the

bad weather, that the huge swells crash in the storm, the foam carried off by the gusting wind, that we might be approaching the
lighthouse at the end of the earth or that Silas Huntly might be our
captain, steering us at breakneck speed toward an unknown, but
doubtlessly terrible fate. It is summer now and there is the danger
of icebergs. Up north, the inland ice of Greenland is calving. The
MS *Kungsholm* follows a safer, southerly course toward America.
There are no icebergs to be seen. I have read about how the
world's largest steamship, the White Star Line's 46,000 ton *Titanic*,
went down on April 15, 1912. But then she took the shortest
route. The passengers in steerage, now called Tourist Class, were
unable to escape from the bowels of the huge steamer. They got
lost. They crammed into the narrow stairways and trampled on
one another. They screamed. Leading the pack, white-bearded old
men in ankle-length black coats came rushing up out of the stair-
wells. Once the steerage passengers had managed to get out onto
the the upper deck and the crowd tried to shove its way to the
Cabin Class area where the lifeboats were, the staff beat them
back. Correctly-clad deck stewards stood guard, keeping the people away while the millionaires were being saved. Screaming and
cursing in all the tongues of Eastern Europe, the crowd found
itself pushed backward. They could be heard shouting, swearing
and praying in Russian, Polish, Yiddish, Hungarian, Romanian and
German. But the Cabin Class passengers had paid as much as
$4,350 for their cabins and had the right to be be rescued first.
That was a lot of money in 1938, more than a year's salary for an
ordinary Swedish professor—but it was even more, several times
as much, back then before the war. That is why almost all those
rescued from the Titanic had paid Cabin Class. Those who could
only afford to pay steerage had no right to a place in the lifeboat.
If you want to ride, it's going to cost you, my friends! And now
these emigrants were swept into the disaster, as the SS *Titanic*
went to the bottom and cold water drowned them.

Here on the MS *Kungsholm*, there was room in the lifeboats even for the Tourist Class passengers. Or perhaps that was just something they said. The emigrants who went down with the *Titanic* would certainly never have bought tickets if they had known that they were going to drown.

We plow along through the big waves and occasionally the water splashes all the way up to where I am standing. I see the green swell and the white foam. Although in reality the wind continues to blow around me and my face is splashed by the great green waves as they break and foam down there, everything suddenly begins to grow silent, a calm comes over me and things seem to move slower. The words come slower. *They trickle.* Then they dry up and stop totally. Behind my ears, the hair at the back of my neck begins to tickle. I feel the tickling spread to my forehead, all over my head, and down my back—like at the barber's. I see everything very clearly, yes, even much more sharply and clearly than usual. Everything is perfectly distinct. I hear everything very clearly in the wind. I know that people are walking by in back of me and that lunch time is long since past. But I can stand here looking down into the water without having to move; everything else slips away and I stand in the middle of a ring of silence. I draw a circle around me where I stand. But I don't move. I am perfectly still, don't form any words, describe nothing. I just watch myself draw the circle, see myself stand down there in it. The whole time I feel the prickly sensation down along my back.

You can stare down into the green whirlpools, falling and tumbling through space the whole time, without moving, without thinking. You know this without words being formed or heard by the ear. You just see. You see your way down and in. And everything floats and changes and is transformed down there. Water sprays and new waves come from far away and are split by the ship and splash up on the face like foam in the wind and put salt in the mouth. But everything stays the same, perfectly still and motionless. You only exist in the glittering pull from down below, and your gaze follows the motion which has no beginning and no end. I think to myself that there is no way I can think my way out of this.

But as I do this, the words return. They are formulated and I recognize them, and the silence is ripped apart. The words are sharp, thorny and tear up my enveloping shield, and then the light and the voices of the people walking back and forth behind me also penetrate. The circle begins to fall apart and the swirls down there lose their attraction. The tickling at my neck is gone, and instead I make the words into a sentence, place sentence after sentence, and in this way build a new circle, but in a different way. Using words, I tell myself that each moment becomes an individual drop falling through time. The falling drop has no limits; it is both beginning and end. And the moments fall past without ever touching one another, because their solitude is boundless, and they fall in an endless stream with neither beginning nor end. Space is a swirling green ocean of drops, each one exactly like the others. And I think to myself that I am thinking this, and that I am thinking this inside just such a drop, in a never-ending waterfall. Since one drop is like the other, I was also in the next drop and the next and the next, and thought the same thought in all of them, and there was nothing which made the next one different from the one before, or that could tell me in which one I was, or when. I am thinking now that I thought the same thing in the last drop, I thought with words, and I thought the same thing in the next drop and the one that followed, and some self capable of knowing in which drop of this endless ring dance some *me* can be found, cannot be distinguished from the others. I can't know which drop I am in, or if I am in all of them at the same time. And the whole time there was the swirling of the green water, the white foam and the waves rolling in from far away, the words that trickled and fell away. Now I just fell and tumbled there by the railing, the hair at the back of my neck prickling, and feeling quivers down along my backbone, across my forehead, cheeks and lips. It wasn't until the sun went down and it began to grow cold that I left. They wondered where I had been. They had looked for me at lunch and in the afternoon, searched all the decks, but had not been able to find me. I knew that they had walked past, but I had drawn a circle around myself and stood perfectly still inside it, so that they hadn't been able to see me. I had let their looking slide off me, had not allowed it to take hold. But I didn't tell them this. I gave them the run-around. I didn't respond to what they said. I let their words slide and spoke of the movie instead. A sign had been put up in the doorway to the First Class Salon announcing that a film was going to be shown that evening. It said: *Movie*.

I can see the sign clearly. It sits on a shiny steel tube stand with three legs. It looks a little like a music stand, but sturdier. The sign is made of thick, cream-colored cardboard. It has a red border and is handwritten in the dashing American style of the thirties, the sort of advertising script known as "film style" and "automobile style," but which doesn't have a real name and now is only used to give a feeling of the thirties to an ad.

Tonight is written in red. Deanna Durbin also has her name in red. Then I see the word *movie*. In black. But I can't make out the name of the movie. It flickers. But I believe it was *One Hundred Men and a Girl*. The truth is that I don't remember a thing about the movie I saw later that evening. I think I can see Deanna Durbin's face, although I never liked her all that much. She would start singing suddenly in the middle of the movie when something was about to happen. But it was the word *movie* that really caught my attention. I can also see it clearly in my mind.

Now that I was emigrating to America, I tried to think in English. Replace the Swedish words with English, and then put them together in the English way. This was also the reason I had taken private English lessons during the spring and early summer from a middle-aged Englishman at his apartment near St. Erik's Square. I took two hours of private lessons everyday except Saturday. Alva said it was so that I would be able to attend American school those years we would be living in New York. She didn't understand what I meant when I spoke of the appearance of different words or when I said that different languages had words with different shapes. That's why I didn't mention to her that the Englishman knew words had particular appearances and linked up with one another in different ways, even though they seemed to mean the same thing.

After my last lesson of the day at school with Miss Rehn, I crossed the asphalt schoolyard and walked down Ålsten Street straight to the streetcar stop. From there I took Number 12 into town. I don't know if there was an elevator in the building. I didn't use it, in any case. I believe he lived two flights up. The windows of his apartment faced the street. He was about fifty and had once had red hair. Now he only had a few gray locks left, and he was bald in the middle of his head like a monk. He had a little moustache and chewed mint candies. He used to wear knicker-bockers, a plaid shirt with a blue silk scarf at his throat and a blue sweater. But the scarf was slightly frayed and the sweater had stains on it.

He came to the door himself to let me in when I rang, but I think he was married, and a couple of times I caught sight of a wife dressed in something brown and heard the padding of slip-pers down the hall towards the kitchen. He invited me in. He was always careful to express himself politely. I, too, was to be polite. Polite, but reserved. Neither pushy nor obsequious.

"It is not good form to be overly familiar in English!"

Then he asked me to sit down and wait for him. He had to finish a lesson. On the round table by the sofa in the hall where I waited, there lay some old issues of *Illustrated London News* from the past winter. He put them there after the family had read them, he said. But he didn't mention the size of the family or anything like that. I didn't generally ask about such things, and didn't ask him, either. But just to be sure, he had informed me at our first lesson:

"It's only in America that people ask personal questions or talk about themselves. There they call each other by their first names and ask as soon as they meet: 'How much do you earn? I'm a ten-thousand dollar man.' Then they tell each other how many times they've been married and how many children they have and how the children are doing in school or if the children are married or divorced and what they do for a living and how much they earn. They tell you if they themselves have ever been millionaires, been elected to public office or been sent to jail for rigging an election, and where they are currently living. And then they say, 'It was great meeting you,' and 'We must get together sometime,' and 'Please come see me.' But they don't mean it. In England, people don't talk like that. There, people respect one another, even if they come from different classes. You should never ask personal questions. This is something you must learn if you want to understand English ways."

I leafed through the magazines and also tried to read the words, while I waited. The USS *Panay* had been bombed and sunk by the Japanese airplanes in the Yangtze River. And *USS* stood for the United States Ship, just as *HMS* stood for His Majesty's Ship or Her Majesty's Ship, depending on whether the regent was King or Queen. One mustn't forget to place the apostrophe correctly to form the genitive. Thus one wrote the *The King's* since there is one, but *the horses'* when referring to more than one horse. Many people are unsure when a word ends in *-s, -sh* or *-z*. They think the apostrophe is placed according to whether the word is singular or plural. That is not the case. It should be *Tom Jones' house* even though he is only one, and it is actually bad form to write *Tom Jones's house,* although it is often written that way, especially in America.

"Do you understand?"

"Yes," I answered, although it wasn't quite true.

In any case HMS *Lady Bird* has been attacked near Wuhu and General Franco's efficient bombers are flying, so that in a single raid on Barcelona 200 people die and 400 are wounded, and there are three pages showing the heavy bombers blowing up the railroad line to Madrid. But when Herr Hitler and Lord Halifax meet and secure the peace of Europe, the magazine writes of *Lord Halifax's visit to Germany.* Perhaps there are other rules for words ending in *-x* or for lords.

I had a long wait that day. General Matsui rode into Nanking with his staff. The war was going well for the Japanese, as was the Spanish Civil War for Franco. But apart from this, the magazines lying on the round table in the hall mostly contained pictures of paintings and drawings, and the like.

I usually had to wait quite a while there in the hall, until the student whose lesson came before my two lessons finished and left. Despite the fact that his other lessons were only forty-five minutes long and that the Englishman was very careful not to let them drag on, I always had to wait. This was because he would retire to the room behind his study and spend a while resting and preparing for his next lesson. In the afternoon these breaks between lessons grew longer and longer. The whole day's schedule was pushed back and he was never able to stay on time. The last student had to wait a long time, and that is what I did every day. But since I was the last student, there was no one waiting to go in when I finished. I also got to spend two full hours with him. His real mission was not to teach me vocabulary, spelling, or how to translate.

"Get yourself a dictionary and a textbook. Listen to the radio for the pronunciation. That'll do it!"

His real mission, he felt—and the reason he spent so much time with me—was to teach me to think in English. We never talked about money. I suppose he sent a bill directly to Gunnar and Alva. But he had never told them anything about this business of thinking in English.

He explained that the most important thing for me was to understand the context of the language. To immerse oneself in a language is not the same as going to a language feast to gather crumbs, even if that is the way Swedish high school teachers approach the subject. They are so Teutonic. He leaned back in his chair, looked up at the ceiling and recited:

"They have been at a great feast of languages and stol'n the scraps. Shakespeare. Love's Labor's Lost. Act five. Scene one. Moth to Costard."

Then he bowed his head, looked down at me and said:

"You will never be able to think in English unless you know your Shakespeare. *By heart!* He *is* the English language."

English was a simplified, blended language. It was an open language. It wasn't rigid like French or bound up in rules like German. That was why it was a good language to work and think with. But for these very reasons, it was important to be able to distinguish between correct and incorrect usage, and to understand the difference. If you know the history of a language, you can begin to think in that language; otherwise, it is impossible.

"In Swedish, one says the four hundreds, but in English, we say the fifth century. That was when the west Teutonic tribes colonized the British Isles and the English language began to evolve. Now that you are going to begin to think in English, you must learn to distinguish several different strata of words. We all possess an Indo-European thought-level. Say two in English!"

"*Two.*"

"In Old English, it is *twa.* It's the same as the German *zwei,* which was previously *zwa,* or like Russian's *dva* or Latin's *duo.*

You can hear that, can't you? In this group you have the words *sister* and *brother* and the words *heart* and *house*. This is our common heritage. There are also the old, old gods. These are words used by people from Bengal to Iceland, not to mention the American and Pacific Areas colonized in the 18th and 19th centuries."

I just nodded. When he began to talk like this, he sat reclining in his chair, his hands clasped behind his neck, and it didn't matter what I said. He spoke without looking at me. Behind him I could see the wall covered in bookshelves. There were dictionaries and bound volumes of periodicals. But I was also interested in what he said. It was as if the languages were woven together before my eyes as he spoke.

"Then come the Germanic words in English. They date from the time the Teutonic tribes freed themselves from the other Indo-European peoples and developed a language of their own. In this group we find words such as *hand,* the English word *hand* as well as the Swedish word *hand,* the English *deep,* which is the Swedish word *djup,* and the English word *sing,* which is the Swedish *sjunga.* You hear how they are related? In this group are words having to do with labor, the sea, colors and everyday life. There are fairy tales and legends. Then, later, you have the Old English words originating on our own islands."

"To the north, up towards Scotland, we then have an additional layer of Scandinavian words. There is the Swedish word *bra* meaning *good,* and *bairn,* the Scandinavian word *barn* meaning *child*. And out around the Shetland and Orkney Islands, English is a rather new language. Norse was spoken there as recently as in the late 18th century. When you switch from Swedish to English, you must reset your brain, just as you must readjust the position of lower jaw when you begin to speak the language. There are three trains of thought—let us call them paths of speech—that you must obstruct, when you begin to think in English. There are several peculiarities in Swedish, but there are three well-worn paths of speech in particular that you must obstruct right from the start."

"First, there is the use of the passive voice. Block that path! You cannot think that way in English. *Jag kallar* in English is *I call*. *Jag kallade* is I called. Go on!"

"*Jag har kallat*, I have called. *Jag skall kalla*, I shall call."

"Watch it! Consider will and shall. But what comes next: *Jag kallas. Jag kallades. Jag har kallats,* and so on? The passive voice is particularly dear to the Scandinavians. In the other European languages, one thinks in a different way. I am called: *jag är kallad*. I was called: *jag var kallad,* and so on. You must place your first roadblock there!"

"The second roadblock concerns the use of the definite article. Here, too, you think differently in Scandinavia. You find it natural to say *en bok, boken, böcker, böckerna*. But actually, it's not natural at all. It is as artificial as everything else in a language. There is nothing natural about words. It is just a method of thought we have agreed upon from one generation to the next. It's just that most people in Europe do it differently than you. They do as we do. *A book, the book, books, the books.* To speak English, you must think along different lines."

"The third thing to be aware of is that Swedish and Latin share something the English, Germans and Dutch don't. We say, 'She loves *her* child, I love *her* child. He has *his* book, I have *his* book.' You can't think like that. You think there is a necessary form which we don't know. You think, "*Jag älskar hennes* (another person's) *barn, hon älskar sitt* (her own) *barn. Jag har hans* (another person's) *bok, han har sin* (his own) *bok*."

When he held forth like this, he spoke in a loud voice, as if he were lecturing a large classroom of pupils. I think he was the one who made me see language as a jigsaw puzzle. Every language had its own rules, and each language had to be treated differently. It isn't enough just to hold your lower jaw and tongue in another way, you have to think differently and see the words link up differently.

"If you ever intend to write poetry in English remember that the words of Latin origin carry a lower emotional current, are of a weaker voltage, than the words that entered into English, or originated in the British Isles before the year 1066. This means that the Latin words brought in by the Church, or even those words brought in earlier by the Romans, also carry a poetic resonance, while those that entered the language after the conquest are generally less powerful, even if they seem very erudite and colorful. You should also avoid using the few Celtic words. They fell out of favor sixteen centuries ago. If you're not sure which word to use, choose the one found in Old Swedish. It usually works! He said all this in English, the words joined together in a manner foreign to Swedish.

I thought a lot about words and how they were linked, as I sat with the *Illustrated London News,* waiting for him to finish his lesson with the pupil who came before me. It wasn't the same person each time. There were three of them, all adults. They weren't women, or high school students. They were men in their thirties. I guessed they were businessmen. They looked that way. They were dressed like businessmen. I no longer remember their faces. I didn't see them; I just noticed that they had creased trousers and handkerchiefs in their breast pockets, and that one of them carried an umbrella although it wasn't raining. But these weren't the only reasons I thought they were businessmen. They couldn't have been government officials, since they would already have known some English and wouldn't have needed to take private lessons. Some sort of English, in any case, although my English teacher said that not even Swedish professors of English spoke the language in a way that would enable them to go in and order a dish of ham and eggs.

"And yet, I'm sure they can analyze *Beowulf,*" he said.

Two of the businessmen came twice a week, while the third was only there on Fridays. "Here in this apartment, we live as in England, with a real *weekend*."

When, after a little while, he opened the door and called me in for my lesson, he had taken another piece of candy. He drank. That was why his face and hands were often swollen. Occasionally, he laughed the way people who drink do. I knew he drank because he was constantly chewing on those strong, transparent mint candies. He would offer me one, too. He kept the candy in a round tin box. There was something written on it, in very ornate lettering, in the style of the previous century. It was printed in garish colors and was highly decorated, with a picture of a four-leaf clover on it. But I don't remember what was written on it, and it's been a long time since I have seen a tin like that.

"These sweets are only made in England," he said.

But I could still smell brandy on him when he leaned towards me, opened a book and breathed in my direction. But I didn't say anything. Nor did I mention it at home. You were not supposed to talk about people who who drank, especially not when my aunts were around. I suppose this was because of Grandfather. One was supposed to pretend that this sort of thing didn't exist. I chewed on the piece of candy and felt it crunch between my teeth. Before I turned to my book, I looked out the window. I could see across St. Erik's Square, toward the bridge leading to Kungsholmsstrand, where I had once lived. But the canal, the shore and the house weren't visible.

He had placed his desk directly beneath the large bay windows, and there he sat in a high-backed, black wooden chair, teaching his students English. From time to time I would catch him, too, gazing out the window. I could see him follow the progress of the blue streetcars. They rattled by down there and he watched them go. He would then forget what he had been talking about, and sit in silence. Behind him was the wall covered with

bookshelves, and further into the room, next to the fireplace and
the big brown, leather armchair and footstool, hung six framed
color prints of men in red jackets chasing a fox. I looked that way,
and one of the mounted men was just about to sound a horn.
Then he picked up his train of thought again and went on as if
there had never been a pause. He leaned towards me as I sat
hunched over the books I noticed a strong smell of brandy again,
and the lesson continued. He lived next to the Lorry. He joked
about it. He told me his friends were always so *surprised* when he
told them that he was going to the lorry that evening. *Lorry* actually meant coach, but in England it was what they called a large
truck. In America, they said *truck* or *motor truck. Truck* was the
older word and had come from Latin, while *lorry* was of more
recent, obscure, origin. But in English, it was called a *lorry,* while
in American—which was just a dialect—it was *truck.*

"In many ways, American is a more old-fashioned language,"
he said.

The joke was that at the Lorry near St. Erik's Square, they
showed movies. It was a movie theater. When he said that he was
going *to the lorry tonight,* he was saying that he was going to the
movies, although it sounded as if he were going to the truck.
When he went to the movies, he said he was going *to the flicks.*
These weren't *flickor* (the Swedish word for girls), it was slang for
going to the movies. Or rather, it was a casual, everyday way of
saying *take in a film.* Among friends one might even say *go to the
flicks* in educated circles. The word *flicks,* of course came from the
fact that the moving pictures flickered a little.

"But you never know," he said. "The Swedish word *flicka* is a
strange word, and we are not quite sure where it came from. It is
related to he Norwegian *fleikja: open up, gape.* So a *flicka* is someone who opens up, who when she lies there, opening and closing, can be said to *flicker.*

When he said this, he chuckled a little at his own joke and put his hand on my shoulder, and I noticed that he smelled very strongly of brandy. He smelled more than usual. He must have drunk a real glass full during the break just before beginning my lesson. It was Friday afternoon, and the brandy fumes hung around him like a cloud. But it was only this one time that he ever placed his hand on my shoulder, and he didn't tell any more of that kind of joke and he really wasn't that kind of person.

Now I see the word *movie* written in black. It is an American word. It isn't even slang. It comes from *moving pictures*. I am going to go to the movies this evening here on board the MS *Kungsholm*, westward bound for New York. I must remember to remove the English words he taught me and to replace them with real American words.

No one goes *to the flicks* in New York, Chicago or Los Angeles, where I am going to live the rest of my life.

C H A P T E R 3

I have gone down to my cabin and into the bathroom. Saltwater gushes out of the faucet. I sit in the bathtub and let the ocean water flow. It is the middle of the day. With my left hand adjust the faucet and in my right I hold a wooden model of the MS Kungsholm. The chief steward in Cabin Class gave it to me when I came on board. It had come in a box and was meant as a souvenir to put on a shelf after the voyage. It was not made to be played with in water. But I had taken it out, locked myself in, filled the tub with water and climbed down into it, even though it was in the middle of the day. It was around noon, May 7, 1915, and I was about to sink the SS *Lusitania* off the southern coast of Ireland, transforming the Great European War into the World War.

The wooden model is white, and it floats and bobs as the warm ocean water pours from the silver faucet. But I picture it as black, with four funnels instead of two. She is the largest ocean liner still in regular passenger traffic across the North Atlantic, in this tenth month of the Great European War. She is the Cunard Line's huge SS *Lusitania,* and now, ceasing her drift, she heads into dangerous waters, even though the promised cruiser escort has failed to show up. Captain William Turner stands on the bridge, heading straight for Queenstown, as if there were no war at all. She's moving at only 17 knots, although the sea is calm and the day sunny, but fog banks are rolling in toward her and Captain Turner keeps the speed down. And he doesn't worry about the escort that has failed to appear nor does he follow a zigzag course to avoid submarines in these waters. I have him stand on the bridge, arms folded across his chest, singing a sailor's song about rolling home, and he beats time on the railing with his fist. Then he continues to smoke and suck on his pipe. He is big and stout, and doesn't understand that there is a real war going on. Or else he has received orders to let the ship be sunk.

All the while, I lay in wait with my U-boat, the U 20, in the water eight nautical miles southeast off Old Head of Kinsale. I am traveling underwater with my periscope up. I observe her. A week ago, on May 1, she left New York with ammunition for the English army fighting the Germans in France. I watch her for a moment, lie in wait for her, creep along like a hungry wolf tracking its prey. I position the U 20 south of her. She is a sitting duck. And then, from a distance of 200 yards, I launch my torpedo.

On deck, the passengers are playing games. They drink tea, and a stout Englishman in a deck chair with a plaid blanket wrapped around his legs is drinking a glass of steaming hot rum, which a steward has just brought him from the veranda cafe on a silver tray. Then the American with the cap who is standing over by the railing looking out at the water shouts:

"Look! Here comes a torpedo!"

A white streak of foam cuts across the heavy gray sea. People rush to the railing. Small children scream. A woman faints. An elderly American woman, her hair tinted blue, shouts:

"My jewels!"

She yanks open the door and is about to fling herself down to her cabin, when the torpedo strikes the starboard side of the ship, up towards the bridge.

Through the periscope I can see how the torpedo hits the ammunition transport, now disguised as a passenger ship. Now she is rocked by a second explosion. The ammunition destined for the western front is sent flying. I give the order to submerge and head north. Our mission is accomplished. The SS *Lusitania* is going to the bottom here, in fifty fathoms of water.

I end my story there. The part with the lifeboats and many victims, I can take another time. That's not as important as firing the torpedo. Not just now. I don't need the saltwater or the model ship for that. I can tell it without props. I often lie down, telling stories with the flip of a steel ball. I toss it up in the air, see it gleam, and catch it, over and over, as I tell my story. If they won't leave me alone, I can sit under a table or up in a tree, and tell my stories there. The only important thing is that no one else is there, and that no one comes to talk, or anything like that.

I know why I chose to tell the story of the *Lusitania.* The MS *Kungsholm* had its own newspaper. In it you could read all the latest news. But there wasn't much about the war. Nothing really about what was happening in Spain. There Franco's troops were called "nationalists," even though they were Italians and Moroccan mercenaries and Germans, and were fascists to boot. But they weren't called fascists here. And there wasn't anything in the paper about the big war coming in Europe. I don't remember any discussion in it about Hitler and Czechoslovakia. It was as though we were at peace.

But wars were raging the whole time. There had been war in Africa, and now there was war in Spain and China. I stood on deck. The day was hazy and gray banks of fog had rolled over the water. Earlier I had been stretched out on a sofa in the library reading. When I finished with Ali Baba and the thieves, I put the book aside in the middle of "The Magic Horse." I had been reading since early that morning and my eyes were tired. I had gone out on deck, passing the bar, where people already stood drinking, and I had turned away and looked out over the glittering ocean rolling in gentle swells beneath the fog. I leaned against the brown teak railing and felt the slow heaving of the ship. Legs wide apart, I stood resting my chin on the damp wood. Out there in the gray mist, where the ocean met the sky, anything could be hiding. There on the port side of the promenade deck, I thought about the bombing in the Mediterranean, about submarine warfare, and about what might happen. Later, when I went down to my cabin and saw the model ship, I remembered that there was real saltwater in the bathtub faucets, too, and that's why I locked myself in, took a bath and told the story of the *Lusitania,* in the middle of the day. I sank the ship in salt water. That time a world war had resulted. They pretended that the ship had not been loaded with ammunition. They sent her into the danger zone so that she would be sunk. Later, all they talked about were the passengers. Many had drowned. Twelve hundred people. And then millions died in the trenches.

I lay submerged in my cabin's bathtub, holding my breath. I had saltwater right up to my eyes, and watched the model as if through a periscope. Once more, I sent a torpedo toward her and sank her again. I came with my hand underwater, grabbed her, and watched as she first raised herself out of the water when the torpedo hit her beneath the bridge on the starboard side, and then went down.

The model was no longer fit for display.

I knew that the *Lusitania* had been transporting ammunition, because it was in the spring of 1938 that I had first become involved in politics. It was then, too, that I really began to read the news dispatches in the papers. I had joined the Young Eagles. This was the Social Democratic children's organization. We weren't supposed to say this, however, since in theory, it was an unaffiliated youth organization. For this reason they referred to it as the Labor Movement's children's organization, and it was led by the Worker's Educational Association. I wore a blue shirt with a red eagle of cloth sewn to its left sleeve, and a red scarf. I can picture my uniform clearly. The odd thing was that I had bought it in the Boy Scout Shop at Tegelbacken. I can still see the shop assistant's surprise when I said that I was a Young Eagle. Of course, I didn't buy the red eagle emblem in the Boy Scout Shop, just the shirt. It's possible that the scouts affiliated with the YMCA wore the same sort of blue shirt as the Young Eagles.

Trying to recall more about my time in the Young Eagles, my memory becomes strangely abstract. The Young Eagles was politics. I lived different existences in different compartments. The school in Ålsten with Miss Rehn and my classmates was life in one compartment. Then I would enter another life in another compartment with Olle and Lennart and the friends I had in Olovslund,

where I used to live. There were others: Kvicksta was one. Neither
Folke, nor Stig, nor the dogs nor even my grandfather really were
part of any of my other lives, although they certainly really existed,
near Mariefred, in Sörmland, Sweden, Earth and the Universe. It
was only I who shifted from one to the other. Those who belonged
in one life would not have recognized me if they had seen me in
another life, another compartment. But perhaps compartment is
not the right word. Sometimes I pictured them as pigeonholes,
open compartments in a giant case; like some sort of printing shop
with various large, open spaces in a flat drawer. Inside each of the
compartments, all one could see were the walls; one couldn't see
from one to the other. But from above one could move a piece of
type from one compartment to another, if one wanted. But I also
saw it as a large, ingenious labyrinth, with numerous passageways
that sometimes tunneled under each other, twisting and turning,
but never running together. It was almost like a twisted ball of
thick yarn or the kind of intestinal system you see when you
remove the cover of an anatomical model. There were passageways that only I knew; places where I was. But I was able to pass
from one existence to another, and back again. The Young Eagles
was another existence.

It was not just the blue shirt and red scarf. It was the politics I
remember. It was Spain and Mussolini and Hitler, and what people
thought about nonintervention. It was more than just words,
telegrams and newspapers. I also went along with the others one
Sunday to collect money for the Spanish people. Perhaps I even
went several Sundays.

We also sang. I know that I once told my son that we had a
small cottage in Judarn Woods, but towards Åkeshovs Estate,
where we used to meet. As I sit here writing this, I am no longer
sure that it really existed. Still, I can picture the room. I sit on a
bench attached to the wall, wearing my blue shirt and red scarf,
and we are singing.

I also remember the posters that hung on the wall. There were three of them. One was of a soldier dressed in gray, against a blood-red background. The soldier holds a hand grenade in his right hand, ready to throw it at Franco's mercenaries. It says NO PASAREIS. It also says CNT and FAI, and it wasn't until many years later that I would wonder what an anarchosyndicalist poster was doing hanging in the clubhouse of a Social Democratic youth organization.

The second poster was of a wounded soldier with a rifle in front of him. The background was black and the uniform a muddy brown. He was obviously in great pain. He was pointing right at you and red blood ran from his temple to the ground. He had already bled so heavily in the dark night that it was clear he was dying. He looked at you and in red letters shouted:

"And you? What are you doing for the victory?"

You understood what he was saying, even though it was written in Spanish.

The third poster showed a clenched fist and airplanes flying up off the paper, heading toward fascist lines. There was a lot of Spanish writing, which I couldn't understand. But I did understand that an air force was needed to defeat the fascists.

However, it is the picture of the dying soldier that remains most distinct. It hung just to the right of the door. You saw it the moment you came in. He pointed at each and every one of us. He raised his head from the pool of blood, looked into my eyes, and pointed at me.

Perhaps he had been the one to make me go to school wearing my blue shirt although I knew somehow that there would be trouble if I mixed one life with the other. I was dressed as usual, when I ate my morning cereal in the kitchen. This was in our new house in Stora Mossen. Mary didn't know what I was planning. I hadn't told her. When I had eaten and had been excused from the table, I returned to my room and changed into my blue shirt and red scarf. I grabbed my book bag, ran down to my bike and took off before anyone could stop me. But I only did this once. It was the morning right after Easter vacation 1938. The classroom fell silent as I entered and sat down at my desk. They didn't want that kind of dress in school. It wasn't suitable, my teacher told me.

I am biking back home at lunch in my blue shirt and red scarf, crossing the Vasterled. I continue up Nyängsvägen and catch sight of the ski slope with its ski jump, and the sheds in the community garden. Up ahead is Bromma Secondary School. The sun flashes in the windows of its long facade. It is newly built of glass and white-plastered concrete. It is rectangular and functional, lacking decoration or color. It might just as well have been a factory, a prison or a modern government office building. The best students in class will be going there in the fall. The school is big, white and austere. It is Sweden's largest school, they say, and right across the street lies our new house. The house was designed by Markelius and all the newspapers have written about it. We had already moved in, even though they were still working on it. It looks like a steamship, with round portholes in the bathroom, a large bridge and teak railing. Here from a distance, the house looks like the secondary school. Glass and white plaster. But I know there are bricks under the plaster and not concrete. This lunch break I am biking past the front of the school. It'll soon be summer and then I'll be going to America, and I'll never, never have to sing their old hymns again. That afternoon, I was once more dressed as the school wished me to be. I was wearing a short-sleeved grey shirt and a knitted tie. All the children stood by their desks and sang:

> What light above the tomb!
> He lives, oh joy!
> Scripture is fulfilled,
> Oh, the height of blessedness!
> Greeted by heaven

He walks in radiance,
The world is delivered,
The victory is his,
The stone is rolled away, the seal broken,
The watchmen have fled from the breath of his Spirit.
And hell trembles.
Halleluia!

I got up with them and sang too. But I sang a different song. It went to the melody of *The Marseillaise*. Nevertheless, I tried to move my lips as little as possible, so that she wouldn't see what I was singing and I kept my voice down, so that I wouldn't really be heard up front. If she had heard me there would have been hell to pay. I sang:

Arise brothers, sisters, dashing youth
Forward! Rally to our banner red!
In battle we would gladly sing
Our song of freedom with the spirit of youth,
Our song of freedom with the spirit of youth.
We swear allegiance to our flag
And so we march to battle
To put an end to injustice,
We will fight on the front line.
Forward, you youthful army!
We're about to make our assault.
Forward! Forward!
You are the vanguard
Rally round our dear red flag.

It must have been in the Young Eagles that I heard about the *Lusitania*. They should take all the presidents, kings, generals and other leaders who want war, fence them in with barbed wire on a large field, and let them fight it out among themselves. But the people had been drawn into a world war. It was that spring I first heard of the Western Front and about the trenches. It was like what was happening in Spain, but much worse. It had gone on for five years.

Another reason it was worse was that neither side was in the right. In Spain, the government was right in fighting Franco, the Italians and the German bombers, but in the World War, there were only the generals, kings, and presidents competing for power, sending people off to die. The *Lusitania* was used as bait. They loaded her with ammunition and then took on all the passengers she could carry, even though the Germans had published warnings in the papers. They didn't provide her with an escort and allowed her to sail slowly, slowly through submarine-infested waters, where the German navy maintained its blockade. They waited for her to be torpedoed, and when it happened, and 1200 people, including 120 Americans, drowned, the Entente could put on a big publicity campaign to bring America into the war.

That's what the generals did when they wanted a war. But where had I heard this? Not from my parents. Not from anyone at school. It wasn't something I would have heard at the Young Eagles. Social Democrats didn't talk like that. It must have been one of the leaders, one who didn't just repeat what the Swedish government said. It must have been an older person. Perhaps someone who was a communist. Or, more likely, a syndicalist. In any case, they became self-evident truths for me, as soon as I heard them. That was the spring Hitler took Austria. I remember the big photograph of Hitler standing in his car, leaning forward and shaking hands with some women. He is back in Braunau am Inn, the place of his birth. He is wearing a trench coat and is smiling. No, he is smirking with delight. And the women jump up and down and want to shake his hand. He has just conquered Austria.

We were celebrating Grandmother's sixtieth birthday in our

new house. The whole family, all the close relatives, were there. Everyone except Gunnar, who was in America. Everyone talked about Austria and about what Hitler was doing to the Jews. We drank coffee in the garden. The house next door, towards Bävervägen, was not yet finished. The scaffolding was still up and the masons were there finishing the facade. Gösta was talking about Hitler, about his sway over the people.

"The masses are stupid, Hitler screams, and the masses stand below him cheering wildly. Heil Hitler! they shout to their leader. Hitler tells them that the masses are like children; one cannot tell the masses the truth. And once more they cheer wildly."

"Well, in that case, they really are stupid!" I say.

Gösta put his coffee cup down and looked at me across the garden table. Then he said:

"What you just said is exactly what Hitler wants you to think and say. Each individual in the crowd looks around and agrees that the masses are stupid, cheering that way when they hear themselves called stupid. That's why the Germans cheer Hitler, who is smart enough to tell it exactly like it is. But the person cheering doesn't realize that it is not just the others who make up the masses, but he, too. And now, here we sit, you, me and the others, and agree that the German masses are stupid, cheering like that when they are called stupid. This way, we fool ourselves. Hitler is crafty. He uses flattery. He tells you that you and he are wise enough to know that the masses are dumb."

Gösta used to talk to me about things like that. He had married into the family. He had once played football for the national team. He was a Social Democrat now, but had been more radical in the past.

"Don't let yourself be fooled," he said.

Then Grandmother told me about a Jewish boy from Austria who was on his way to America with his parents when he fell ill on board ship. They realized it was infantile paralysis and that he had caught it from eating an improperly rinsed apple. The only place the boy could be cured was Germany, so the whole family, which had packed up, been allowed to depart and leave for a new home in America, had disembarked in England, to take the boy back to Germany for treatment. When the family arrived back in Germany, they were met at the border station by the police, who carried them off the train and took them away. They were Jews and had no right to be in Germany or travel there, and so they were thrown in prison.

"Did the boy die?" I asked.

"I don't know," answered my grandmother. "Perhaps the boy was later taken to a prison hospital."

I wonder where she heard or read that story. She wasn't in the habit of talking politics. That was one of the many stories going around. A week later I was back at Kvicksta and there were no political discussions. I don't remember hearing about China or Spain, Mussolini or Hitler, or anything like that from summer 1938, and no one spoke of Jews, or anyone else, trying to escape. That was the last summer without war. I had taken many books with me to read. Most of them were on technical subjects. A Frenchman had recently designed a plane anyone could build and fly. It was called the Flying Flea. It was banned in Sweden that year, I think. You could crash it. But I had saved my money to buy a book of plans and descriptions of people who built the Flying Flea and flew it. I could lie on the floor in the corner room for whole days and picture myself building the plane. In the yard I drew the shape of the wings in the gravel. I measured carefully and followed directions to the letter. In America, I would also fly.

At the end of this last summer at Kvicksta, just before we were to leave for New York, I returned home to our house at the corner of Bävervägen and Nyängsvägen, across from Bromma Secondary School. I stood in the late summer sun, up on the veranda, leaning over what looked like a ship railing, here at Nyängsvägen 155, and

watched the others bicycling to school at the start of the fall semes-
ter. They arrived in large flocks. They filled the entire street, all the
way from the Västerled to the big white school building. There
were so many of them that it wasn't even forbidden to ride several
abreast. They swung into the schoolyard and dismounted at the
bike park. Directly below me passed those without bicycles, on
foot. I watched them as they crossed the street down there, heading for the school doors. There were beginning students (fifth-
graders) in shorts, wearing for the first time newly-purchased
school caps which they had not yet managed to break in. There
were older boys, who wore knickerbockers and soiled school caps,
heavily creased. I watched the fifth-grade girls tripping along, and
the bare-headed senior high school students, who were almost
adults. I recognized many. But I was no longer one of them.

I am now leaving them, I thought. I hung over the teak railing
and observed those remaining behind. Back in Stockholm I had
begun reading the newspapers again, and the war had returned.
They'll be left here in Europe, in the war, I thought. Now, two
weeks later, as I walk through the corridor on A-deck and up the
wide stairway, I remember Grandmother's story about the Jewish
boy. He hadn't escaped.

Out on deck the sea wind is raw and cold. The water looks
gray and dark. There is foam on the heavy swells. I hang over the
railing, a taste of salt in my mouth. After a while I go into the
library. There is still no one there. I have finished the fourth volume of *One Thousand and One Nights* and have begun the fifth.
This dark chilly day I lie on the leather sofa reading about Sidi
Numan, who marries a beautiful woman, only to discover that she
spends her nights visiting the cemetery, where, in the company of
ghouls, she digs up and eats recently-buried corpses. For making
this discovery, his wife punishes him by turning him into a dog,
but he meets a good woman who gives him back his human form
and helps him take revenge on his evil wife by changing her into a

mare, which he beats everyday. The story is full of magic and remarkable things, but it is not really exciting. I have a hard time picturing it as I read. It is just words. I hurriedly read on in *One Thousand and One Nights*, however. It is already afternoon, September 8, which is why I rush through the stories here in the library without being really interested anymore. I have to read fast, because I only have tomorrow left. Then we will arrive in New York. I have made up my mind to read all six volumes before we get there.

CHAPTER 4

t isn't strange that I didn't remember if I had eaten breakfast that morning I read about Sinbad. I don't remember any of the meals on board the MS Kungsholm. That is, I know meals were served, and I also know that I ate an American breakfast including a bowl of shredded wheat. I know there was strawberry ice cream, and that you could have seconds and thirds (although I think I remember that some of the adults around me began to protest). But I don't remember anything about the meals themselves. I do remember the call signaling meals. A gong sounded and the passengers in their deck chairs looked at their watches and some of them began to get ready. They got out of their chairs, wandered toward their cabins and then took the elevator down to the dining room. It was like being on the train, when white-clad waiters walked along the corridor announcing that the first sitting was served and people got up.

In Cabin Class on this ship, the ladies and gentlemen ate together while the children and servants ate by themselves. Those eating in the Cabin Class dining room at eight dressed for dinner. Notice was given in English, *Evening Dress*. It wasn't said in Swedish. A tie and jacket was sufficient for lunch. But I don't remember this clearly.

Actually, I should have been eating with the adults, since I was eleven going on twelve. According to the rules it was only children under ten who had to eat with the servants. I also had a tie. But at our house, the adults always ate by themselves. Otherwise they would not have been able to talk without being disturbed. They also ate different food.

I can picture the table, however. I am sitting in a soft chair with armrests. There is a pillar nearby and the table is round. The linen is spotless and newly pressed. Woven into the white damask tablecloth is the three-crowns, the logo of the Swedish American Line. Someone leans toward me and asks something. In the center of the table is a vase with freshly-cut flowers. The vase is silver. The napkin on my plate is artistically folded. It stands straight up like a fan. The tree crowns also gleam out from the napkin. The table is elegantly set, I see. The silverware with the three crowns is polished and heavy. A fish fork and a meat fork lie to the left of the plate; to the right lie a soup spoon, fish knife and meat knife; above the plate there is a dessert spoon, fruit fork and fruit knife. There are two glasses, one large and one small, in front toward the right side. They glisten and sparkle. Both are decorated with the three crowns of the Swedish American Line. I know that I carefully examine the eating utensils. I can't use a knife. I don't know how. When I ate in the kitchen at home, the food was cut for me, so that it wouldn't take long. For the most part I generally didn't eat things that needed to be cut. And so I wouldn't stick my fingers in the food on those occasions when I ate with the grown-ups, Alva had the silver pusher put out for me. I associate it with the dining room. I am not allowed to use it in the kitchen. It is like a little rake one uses to get the food up on the fork. The adults eat with knife and fork. They turn the fork, and with the help of the knife they push the food onto the fork. I have never met any other boy who had to eat with a pusher. Not that he could remember, and not now as an eleven-year-old, in any case.

This is why, when I stayed for dinner at Olle and his brother's house, I sometimes pretended to have an injured hand. That was the reason I had to eat with my right hand only, I said. That way I didn't have to reveal that I couldn't eat with both knife and fork like the others. Or else, when they were having fish, which I couldn't bone without using my fingers, I told them the doctor had advised me to avoid it. I got a rash from fish, I said. To make this sound better, I said: no fish, eggs or strawberries.

This is what I told them when I ate at Olle and Lennart's in

June, after school let out, before they left for the West Coast. Olle's
mother had made boiled pike perch. I told them how I broke out
in big red blotches on my arms. The eruptions looked something
like hammers and clubs. They appeared suddenly. Then they
spread. And itched. I also broke out in a fever. I went on like this,
while all of them sat there cutting their fish, removing the backbone and placing it at the edge of their plates. Then they ate the
delicious white fish-meat with melted butter, chopped hard-boiled
egg and fine newly-peeled potatoes. But I didn't let on about anything, and took bread and unpeeled potatoes. I had also said that I
always ate unpeeled potatoes because there were so many nutrients just below the skin. Nutrients which were lost when the peel
was removed. That is why I now sat at the dining table in Olle and
Lennart's house, chewing the thick, bitter peel of last year's potatoes, a smile on my lips, and saying that I liked it. It was good. But
I also chattered on like this to avoid speaking of other things. Olle
had not been accepted by Bromma Secondary School, and I had. I
hadn't thought it necessary to apply, but Gunnar felt that I should,
to see if I was good enough or not.

"One mustn't run away," he had said.

One morning I crossed Nyängsvägen, from the house to the
school, to look at the list of those who had been admitted. It had
been posted on the door. My name was on the list. Jan Myrdal was
to begin in class in the fall. But Olle's name wasn't there. He had
not been admitted. I was going to America, however, and needn't
have applied. I didn't mention this to Olle's parents. Instead, I told
them how sick fish made me. It had been Olle's mother who, with
a smile, had corrected me once when, after eating dinner at their
house, I had gone up to her, shook her hand and thanked her the
way grandmother had taught me.

"In better families, one doesn't thank the hostess that way!"

I never forgot that. I thought about it as I sat there at her table
chewing on the coarse peel of last year's potatoes.

I knew how to eat soup though. You mustn't slurp. No sound should be heard when you eat. Therefore, you shouldn't bang the spoon against the bowl either. You shouldn't shove the spoon all the way into the mouth; one should slowly sip the soup from the spoon and and silently swallow it. You shouldn't tip the soup bowl or pull the spoon towards you to scrape out the last drops. The spoon should be moved away from the body. The spoon should be held as if it were a newly-sharpened pencil with a long, narrow lead you were supposed to write with without breaking the point. This is what Alva had told me when I ate with the adults.

"Try not to be so unaesthetic," she had said.

In the kitchen, however, I ate as usual, the way you eat cereal. Now I examined all the eating utensils, the many knives. I understand the system and can describe it, but I can't work it. I wonder if it is noticeable from the other tables. I think through what I am about to do. That's why I still remember how the table is set. This must be the first real meal we have eaten on board. But I don't remember who the other people at the table were.

I look away from the table setting, up towards the ceiling. There are real flowers in a huge wreath up there beneath the silver cupola. Painted figures wander around, there above the flower arrangements. Bare-breasted maidens. Some of them are harvesters. They carry baskets of grapes on their heads. Others are planters and are sowing, while still others are fisherwomen, pulling in nets. And then there are those who just stand there staring off into the sunset. But they are all bare-breasted. They wear wide skirts. They sweep with their skirts as they walk around the room above the tables. They swirl their skirts and thrust out their breasts. I look at their breasts, pretending that I am just absentmindedly staring off into space. Through my bad eye, the girls are almost invisible. But the colors are warm and I can just make out the figures and can imagine them walking, and almost see them as they swing and swish their skirts. With my good eye, however, I see the girls clearly, distinctly. They stand perfectly still against the silver ceiling, and I can even see their eyes and nipples. But the colors are different through this eye: cold. There are also men in the painting, but the men are not as interesting. They dig in the ground, carry things and walk about. They appear to be wearing some sort of swim suit. But the girls are beautiful, especially one who holds her right arm at her hip. She has flowers in her hair and looks right down at the audience and smiles a little and thrusts out her breasts. She has long black hair which the wind has caught. If I suddenly switch eyes to look at her, I can see her hair flutter, and then she moves. Her one breast is visible from the side and the other from the front, and she has red, red lips and a full white skirt of some thin, almost transparent cloth. I squint and try to look like I'm thinking about something special, about the crossword puzzle we had discussed, or about the weather, which they say is taking a turn for the worse—all so as not to be noticed staring at her. I see her at night, too, when I am all alone in my cabin.

In my memory, the MS *Kungsholm* is, for the most part, a ship empty of people, these first ten days of September 1938. I catch a glimpse of people in the bars, faceless figures sit in deck chairs, a blurred crowd might be seen over in the salon. But with the exception of a few sharply chiseled, clearly visible scenes, the eleven-year-old wanders up the stairs and along the corridors in solitude. Alone he stands looking at the birds in the big cage, while gray, motionless figures are dimly seen in the bar to the left, and a group of faceless people sit frozen around the middle table in the game room to the right. The clink of ice from the left and the mumbling from the right have fallen silent and died away; the only thing to be heard above and beyond the sound of the engines is the bird song, which grows louder and louder. But I can no loner see the birds. It's the eleven-year-old I see. The checked, short-sleeved shirt, which had lost its top button, is held together at the throat by a striped red and gold tie. The tie has a sauce stain, which he has tried to remove with soap and cold water. But the stain can still be seen. He's wearing long pants. Gray flannel. They are unpressed, even though he lays them under his mattress each night to give them a crease. His brown shoes are scuffed. His shoelaces are in pieces tied together and the heel of his right shoe is worn down on one side. He wears out shoes that way. He stands leaning forward, staring at the birds, his hands shoved deep into his pockets. He thinks about Africa and South America, about vine-hung jungles and Johnny Weissmuller, swinging from tree to tree in the movie *Tarzan*, which he has seen. He shouts in a loud voice so that all the animals can hear him, and he moves the palm of his hand back and forth in front of his mouth, turning his shout into a mightly trill, heard throughout the jungle. He doesn't really do this. He just imagines the mighty roar that rises above the floor of the jungle and keeps his hands in his pockets and his mouth closed. Then he turns and walks toward the spacious men's lounge, the smoking room, to take a look at Manhattan. When he enters the smoking room he has to turn once more in order to see the mural. The clock above the door shows New York time. Manhattan in its enormity, as seen from the sea, is depicted here on the wall, and the perfect skyscrapers rise like some man-made mountain range above the water. In the foreground an ocean-going steamship churns along across the entire picture. It is so beautifully painted that it causes him to shiver.

Now I know it was Kurt Jungstedt who painted this panorama. I like his work. Later on, his watercolors would provide me with my image of Zola's France. I have tried to get hold of a real reproduction of his MS *Kungsholm* work, but haven't been able to find one. But that September forty-five years ago I stand there looking at the large picture. And I know that as long as I live, I will live there in New York. It is the most beautiful city in the world: skyscrapers, the sea and the sky.

I don't know if there were others in the smoking room while I

stood there studying the view of New York. But this feeling of solitude continues day after day. The eleven-year-old does not inhabit
a populated world as he wanders through this great floating city
there is a void around him.

I am going down to do laps in the swimming pool. It's at the
very bottom of the ship, on F-deck, below the dining room. It is
quite a good-sized pool. Not as big as the one in the Sports Palace,
where I usually went swimming when I still lived in Stockholm,
but big enough for being on a ship. It must have been almost six
meters wide and twelve or thirteen meters long. I come from the
sauna. I've only been there a very short time. I wash my feet on a
foot sponge, shower, and then dive into the water. It is cool and
salty. Then I swim 30 meters. I have decided to swim half a kilo-
meter. I turn and twist around like a seal each time I reach the
side. It doesn't take very many strokes. I push off the tile with my
feet and then shoot away. Each time I kick off, I count.

"That's the thirty-eighth. And now for the thirty-ninth...."

When I've kicked off for the fortieth time, I reckon I have done
my five hundred meters.

But I don't remember if there was anyone else in the swimming pool. I can see myself swimming, and although it doesn't
seem possible, it's as if I were alone there. I sit on the edge for a
moment dangling my feet in the water. I am out of breath. Then I
go in and take a look at the gymnastics equipment. There are
mechanical horses that jump when you sit on them, rowing
machines, and exercise bicycles where you can sit and pedal as
fast as you can. You can change gears and bike uphill to exert
yourself, and you can see how fast you are cycling and how far
you have gone, without ever having left the spot. But I'm alone
there, too. And it's the same in the elevator going up.

This did not surprise me at the time; that's just the way it was. I
wonder about it now though, forty-five years later. I observe the
eleven-year-old boy who wanders through the ship and along the

deck, who lies on the leather sofa in the library, trying to finish *One Thousand and One Nights*, and I think I understand what this absence of people means. On this voyage he is changing lives. He says it himself in the smoking room of the MS *Kungsholm* (on this her seventy-first voyage west) in the middle of the North Atlantic, as he stands before Kurt Jungstedt's panorama of New York:

"That's where I'll live the rest of my life."

He thinks this clearly as he sits by the swimming pool on F-deck, and remembers the Sports Palace in Stockholm.

"That's where I used to go swimming, when I lived in Sweden."

CHAPTER 5

There were different worlds on board the MS *Kungsholm*. But the ship was so ingeniously planned that they never met. It might seem that our Cabin Class was the entire universe. We moved around in what seemed unlimited freedom, through corridors, stairways and salons. It was only later that we gradually came to realize there were doors where the glassed-in veranda ended. Doors which led out of Cabin Class. But these were shut. Most passengers did not even notice them. When I looked out the porthole in my cabin, however, I could see the Tourist Class passengers walking out on their deck. They moved around at the top of their other world.

There were doors leading down there. I think they were located aft, in the stairwell leading down from B-deck. I remember them as closed, white doors. Closed, yet unlocked. These were off limits. It was forbidden to leave your class. You couldn't get permission from the steward, or even the head steward. Only the crew on duty could move between lower and upper class. Off duty, the crew lived by themselves, in a world apart. To enter there was even more prohibited. The first days on board I walked by those closed doors. *NO ENTRANCE*, it said. On the third day I looked to see if they were really locked. I can see myself on the stairs; I try the brass handle, see the white door open and look down the corridor of this other world. I hurry away as a steward approaches from the distance. The white door leading to the other world is shut once more and I slowly walk towards the wide stairway. Opposite there one finds the purser. It says *PURSER'S OFFICE* in small gold letters.

If you wished to leave your class through the forbidden doors, you had to seek special permission from the purser himself. He had a uniform with three wide gold braids on a white background on his sleeve. He was powerful within his jurisdiction, just as the chief petty officer was in his. The chief wore four gold braids on a violet field, but I had never seen him. Only the captain outranked them. The captain not only had the right to marry and bury at sea, but could also place anyone he wanted in chains and keep his prisoner locked up in the ship's own brig. In the evening he would open the small window, looking in with a chuckle on the wretches who lay there on beds of old straw. The captain had the right to shoot anyone who disobeyed his orders.

"Get back!" he shouted, "Get back, you dogs!"

And then he pulled out his six-shooter and fired straight into the mob.

Even if the captain went stark raving mad, he was still unimpeachable. And now, as he stood roaring drunk in the sunshine on the bridge, his gold embroidered cap-peak cracked, his uniform jacket, its four broad gold braids stained with red wine, hanging loose over his shoulders, his shirt unbuttoned, revealing a glistening red and blue eagle tattooed across his hairy chest, even now, as he stood bawling and singing, marking time in the air with his schnapps bottle, he was still in command, still the absolute leader.

With an evil glimmer in his small yellow eyes, eyes hidden beneath drooping bush eyebrows, he ordered the MS *Kungsholm* to set a course for the South Pole, and to head south towards the equator. The first mate, who anxiously cleared his throat and looked for a minute as though he were going to challenge the order, had to duck when the captain threw his empty bottle in his direction.

"Does the first mate want to say something?" the captain growled.

The first mate opened his mouth several times and shut it

again, like a fish out of water. Finally he clicked his heels together, saluted, and went off to carry out the captain's order. And the MS *Kungsholm* bore south towards an unknown fate. Down below, sheltered from the rough weather, we passengers all wandered anxiously about, wondering and whispering to one another in the corridors. Not even the rotund, balding ammunition mogul from Bofors could persuade the first mate to throw the captain in irons and take over command. The mate recoiled when he heard the suggestion and ran off, his hands covering his ears. As I came up out of the large hall and walked toward the promenade deck, I told myself that there was no way the MS *Kungsholm* could avoid sharing the fate of the three-masted *Chancellor*.

I stood on the promenade deck, my back to the railing and my arms folded across my chest, observing them there as they slept in their deck chairs, while the sun shone from a blue sky; they were not yet aware of the approaching catastrophes. A few of them turned uneasily in their sleep, now as the shadow slid from their faces, with the sun's sudden shift in the sky at this abrupt change of direction. They woke up and jerked upright, terror shining from their wide-open eyes as they realized that the MS *Kungsholm* had changed course. Smiling grimly, I looked into their future. I saw which of them would be the first to be eaten when times turned bad, when the survivors of the MS *Kungsholm's* terrible fate drifted along in lifeboats without oars or provisions far from any trade route, in the empty expanses of ocean down along the Tropic of Capricorn south of Saint Helena. The fat, bald cannon-king from Bofors (who had caused the final catastrophe by hiding 50 kilograms of nitroglycerin in his baggage) held out his white hands in supplication after he drew the fatal lot, when the chief petty officer got the knife and the hungry crew licked their lips.

Sometimes in the evenings, on this the MS Kungsholm's final voyage, we could see the first mate standing at the railing on the starboard side. Watching the sun sink in the west, he seemed lost in sombre thoughts as the vessel relentlessly kept to its southerly course. In a whisper we would confide our anxiety to the first mate, and he would look straight at us, point out that he was just a god-fearing son of a fisherman from Bohuslän, out to do his duty, and that our words in themselves were a crime. It was not until the vessel sailed into the enormous seaweed beds of the Sargasso Sea, just west of longitude 45 degrees west and latitude 30 degrees north, the captain keeping to his southerly course, that the first mate sighed heavily and took upon himself the momentous responsibility of trying to seize command.

Now the Sargasso seaweed threw its tentacles around our ship. The long ropes of seaweed, which until then had floated past in the clear, extraordinarily transparent sea, bunched together more and more, eventually forming islands into which the ship pushed and became entangled. The decaying vegetation constituted a vicious, foul-smelling gruel. The sun beat down unmercifully and the tar melted. The captain stood on the bridge. He spoke to the crowd which poured up out of the ship, which now stood screaming, arms uplifted down on the foredeck. The captain shouted that he had come to deliver them and to lead them out of the calm of the Sargasso Sea. He asked if they trusted him and if they were prepared to follow him to the ends of the earth. The crowd down below cheered wildly. Slowly now, the first mate crept up behind the captain, his dagger raised. The blade flashed in the sun. Just then the deck stewards appeared. It was time for five o'clock tea. The passengers, wrapped in their deck blankets, sat up in anticipation, and I turned away, placed my hands on the railing and looked out over the ocean and ended my story about the fate of the MS *Kungsholm*.

That was the afternoon the American university student came up from Tourist Class. I remember this because when I had finished my story about the sinking of the MS *Kungsholm*, I went astern. They sat there in the winter garden in their wicker chairs, Gunnar, his assistant and the student. That was when Gunnar spoke about the World's Fair. It was going to take place in New York the next year, and Markelius was working on the Swedish pavilion. The Future and Democracy were to be the central themes of the fair.

"The central element, the focal point of the New York World's Fair is going to be the presentation of Democracy City," he said. "America wants to show the strength of democracy."

This was to be a Roosevelt-era world's fair. That is why Sweden should take the money it was going to throw away on the pointless Tokyo Olympics (which thank heavens the Japanese had cancelled) and use it to really show what Sweden had accomplished in the socio-political sphere. That would be significant. Sweden had a near monopoly on American goodwill now. This should be taken advantage of. Millions of people would visit the fair. It would be helpful to Roosevelt in his effort to overcome America's problems.

The university student was traveling on the cheapest ticket. He had spent half a year in Stockholm. He was a sociologist. He had come up to Cabin Class to talk with Gunnar. He wanted to discuss Swedish population policy. He had written a paper on it. I think he was going to Harvard. He had been greatly influenced by Gunnar, he said. From then on, he was up in Cabin Class every day.

Gunnar had been at Harvard earlier that year to receive an honorary degree and had lectured on the population question in relation to democracy. There was a truly intellectual atmosphere at the university, he felt.

"The young social scientists there aren't narrowly specialized in the German way; they have perspective and a solid educational background."

I thought I remembered the student's name (I should), but I

don't. But I can picture him. He looked like the typical American student in the advertisements. Tall and lanky, with sandy hair. He laughed a lot. He must have been with us the entire crossing, but in my memory he is associated with the very last day.

Or, to be exact, there are two parallel versions. In the first, he was only there that single day, and in the second, he was there for the entire crossing. In the latter version, he usually sat with Gunnar and Gunnar's assistant, talking. The deck stewards treated him as if he belonged in Cabin Class, but his cabin was at the bottom of the ship. I went down with him once. He opened the forbidden door as if he had the right.

"Never ask permission," he said.

It was crowded there on the other side. The cabins were small, four berths in each.

But the fact is that I also used to wander about down there on my own, during the entire trip. If one just managed to cross over between classes without being seen at the door by some steward, no one would say anything. I wasn't noticed as I walked about. Nor did I look any different from the boys down there. But even if a steward saw me, he would say nothing as long as I kept walking toward him and didn't look aside.

Gunnar talked about America and the student agreed. The student was a New Deal Democrat. Gunnar was of the opinion that Roosevelt was a genuine leftist, America would now succeed in solving its problems. The New Deal was an expression of the democratic tradition of Yankee idealism: not allowing oneself to be fettered by prejudices and antiquated concepts, looking at things with fresh eyes, and then doing what had to be done and working hard, with no reward other than one's own good conscience.

"Roosevelt's young advisors are competent and honest. They are professors, coming from research libraries and lecture halls, and are not local politicians from the small, smoke-filled backrooms where members of the political machine used to make their deals in the old Tammany-Hall fashion. There are now ten to twelve million unemployed. Roosevelt realizes that this situation is unnecessary in a country that is an entire continent, with all the natural resources of a continent. It is just a matter of seeing to it that the petty, local special interests, the remaining conservative civil servants, and the central bank system, do not put a damper on the coming boom, that the high level of business activity is allowed to absorb the masses of unemployed. Roosevelt is trying to break with traditional conservative stinginess."

I can still see them seated at the round table in the winter garden. Gunnar is smoking. He isn't talking with them, he is talking to them the way he does to journalists and students.

"America," he said, "America is *the new Athens.* And like Athens, it is not without its great inequalities. But for the scientists, America is the New Greece. You possess a broad outlook and a thirst for knowledge not to be found in Europe. Just look at the fields of medicine and natural sciences! But this is particularly true of the social sciences. That's because of the openness, the amiability and the pragmatic idealism of the American people. There is a hospitable, tolerant curiosity in America, perhaps originating in the Puritan heritage. As you know it was from the narrow-mindedness of the Old World that the first Americans fled."

I can see them sitting there and hear them talking, and I should be able to remember the student's name. I should know for sure whether I saw him just that one time on the boat or whether it was for an entire week. After all, I know him. His family lived in upstate New York, near Syracuse, and he had a younger brother my age. I visited them over a weekend, just after our arrival in New York.

"But of course you should go," Gunnar said. "That's how Americans are: hospitable and open."

But even as I sat on the train heading north, I wondered if I had really been invited. I wondered if the student had meant what he said as a serious invitation, or if he was just being polite. The Englishman, from whom I had taken private lessons that spring, had warned me expressly about this objectionable American habit of tossing out an invitation to visit their homes, in the middle of a casual conversation.

"And then they say, 'It was wonderful meeting you,' and *'Look me up* when you come,' and 'I really hope you'll come and see me.' But when you finally stand there at their door, you realize that they hadn't meant anything by it and that it had just been a lot of words. In America, an invitation is no invitation," he had said.

And if, in fact, the student had really meant it as an invitation, was it actually just hospitality, or was it that he was after a recommendation by Gunnar for a fellowship, or for Gunnar to put in a good word for him? But I hadn't shown what I was thinking or said anything about it. If I had said anything like that, Gunnar would have been furious. He would have said that I was thinking like an upper-class brat, like a European.

"You aren't worthy of being in America!"

Gunnar had not even asked me if I wanted to go, when the student said that it would be nice if I could come up and see them sometime, and that he had a brother my age. Gunnar just accepted for me right there at the round table, before I had a chance to answer. He didn't even look at me. He ran his fingers through his hair like a real American professor, smiled at the student and said:

"That's excellent. It's really very kind of you to look after Jan for a few days. You're taking the train straight home when we arrive in New York, aren't you? We'll send Jan up on Monday then, so you'll have time to unpack and put things in order before he arrives. He won't be any great bother. He pretty much takes care of himself. You can send him back on Friday, that is, if you want to keep him that long."

"It'll be a pleasure," said the student.

Gunnar took out a package of Lucky Strikes from his coat pocket

It was yellow and green, with black letters inside a red circle. It was unopened. He pulled off the cellophane wrapper and pulled up the tinfoil in the corner. Then he knocked up a cigarette with his thumb, pulled it out and returned the package to his pocket. The student got out his matches. He hurried. It was a matchbook bearing the Swedish American Line's three gold crowns. The first match he struck wouldn't light. Gunnar waited, the cigarette in his hand. The second match flared. The student leaned forward, held the burning match in his right hand while protecting the flame with his left, and offered the light. Gunnar took a deep drag, exhaled the smoke through his nostrils and said:

"That way we can get settled in our new apartment, too. And Jan doesn't start school until the following week. That way he doesn't have to loaf around. And right from the beginning he'll get to see another part of America, besides New York City. That's a great idea. It was very kind of you."

"It'll be a pleasure," said the student. "My parents will be pleased."

This conversation must have taken place at afternoon tea, Friday, September 9, 1938. We were due to arrive in New York the next day. I stood there a moment, looking at them. But they had stopped paying any attention to me. Nothing more was said of my visit to the student's home. They spoke about Russia. In any case, Nazism was worse.

I left them and went aft to the smoking room. I stood there a long time, in front of the panorama of Manhattan. Once again it was as though I were all alone. The murmuring at my back died away. The figures around the tables froze, grew misty and faded away. All that was left was the dull, rhythmic sound of the engines and the sensation of the slow heaving floor beneath my feet. There was sun on the water and a blue sky above the towering buildings.

"The skyline!" I said to myself, *"The skyline!"*

CHAPTER 6

Through the light sleep of morning, I notice that stillness has settled in around me and that the MS Kungsholm is behaving differently. I step out of a dream, which vanishes behind me as I wake. I know there is something I told myself that I had to remember, but upon waking only the contours remain, and they, too, fade as I open my eyes. When I close my eyes again and try to recapture them, they are gone. It is only with the help of words that I know they were there. But I wasn't fast enough to capture them with words, either. Maybe they couldn't be formulated in words. This had not been a bad dream. A feeling of a spring morning remains in the body, with open windows and white curtains that blow into the room, billowing and waving, of window-catches that tug in the wind, and outside, a wide-open sky with small, fleecy ribbons of cloud way up high, and black woods far across the meadow. But I don't know if that is what I have been dreaming about. I don't think it was. It's just a feeling I have in my body. The dream was different. It went further and opened out into some other direction.

As I lie in my berth, eyes wide open, I notice that the engines sound different from before; the ship is also rolling in another way.

"We are here," I say.

I throw off my blankets and jump out of bed. I look out the porthole but so far all there is to see is the morning fog on the water. We are lying at anchor waiting for the fog to lift. I look out into the mist. It's already growing lighter and thinning. I see the map before my eyes. We are lying in Lower New York Bay, and over there is Staten Island. Soon we will pass through the Narrows, in towards Upper New York Bay. Suddenly the map grows so clear in the fading morning mist that it is as if etched in glass. I see Staten Island's fading shoreline, Brooklyn opening its jaws, thrusting the lower part towards Coney Island and up ahead the Manhattan skyline. For one short moment, the lines seem clearly engraved on the mist. But even as I try to see in the direction of the New Jersey shore, beyond Staten Island, they fade and are gone completely, and I just remember how the map looked. Now we are moving again, inward bound.

I eat a real American breakfast that morning. I put two buckwheat pancakes on my plate. I place a round ball of butter in the middle of each. Then I pour maple syrup over the melting butter and the brown buckwheat cakes. This tastes like nothing I have eaten in the old country. Silently, I speak to myself in American words.

"Maple syrup," I say. Actually, it should be called maple sap, since it is sap of the sugar maple and not syrup. *"Butter,"* I say in English. *"Pancakes of pure buckwheat,"* I say. But I pretend not to be saying anything at all. When someone speaks to me, I just grunt in response. But in that too, I am American. These are noises foreign to the Swedish language. I write them in my mind at the same time as I answer with them. They are also found in books written in English:

"Eh! Eh? Ooooooh. Mmm."

It's possible to get through an entire conversation in English just by grunting in various ways, and if you don't know what to say, you just mumble "er . . . " and clear your throat. I knew this not just from having read books, I had also heard it at the movies, when I had seen American films.

We are on our way through the Narrows. They are talking to me, telling me to hurry up, to do or not do this or that, and I just grunt in reply, there at the breakfast table. But inside I'm talking with American words, talking about what I am eating for *breakfast,* and I tell myself that I *soon shall arrive at New York.*

I go up to the promenade deck after breakfast and pay no attention to the Statue of Liberty or the lowlands over on the Jersey side, but just lean over the starboard railing. It's a sunny day, with clear air and a blue sky, and up ahead Manhattan climbs out of the water. The skyscrapers rise above the city. Although they're still far-off, I think I see the windows flash in the morning sun. The Upper Bay is filled with ships, freighters, ferries and tugs. A great ocean liner is outward bound. It is already on its way out to sea. It appears to be black with white decks, and something golden gleams on the funnel. But it is far behind us. I don't see any other *liners* at the arrival *dock*.

From the direction of Governor's Island, a ferry approaches. We are going to cut across its path. We are heading toward the Hudson River, and it is on its way from its terminal, down by the Battery at the southern tip of Manhattan, to St. George, on Staten Island. As it nears, I see that it is a large ferry. But we are bigger. People on board the ferry wave to us and I wave back. I see that the name of the boat is Miss New York. Once they pass I have a clear view. I look up the East River toward the bridge. This is the Brooklyn Bridge. And now Manhattan is right there; the skyscrapers rise, tower upon tower, clean and bright against the blue sky. It is more than a forest of buildings, it is a mountain range of them. In the clear morning air, I see the pinnacles rise, ridge upon ridge, north across Manhattan.

Up ahead the morning sun is reflected from thousands and thousands of windows. There's the Chrysler Building, and that one there must be the Empire State Building, the world's tallest. I don't know the names of the smaller skyscrapers, but I am finally seeing Manhattan's skyline in person.

The MS *Kungsholm* continues its journey up the Hudson River and Manhattan's waterfront lies against the light. Shading my eyes with my hand, I see the silhouette of the Woolworth Building in the haze, beyond the rows of piers and their ships. Ferries shuttle back and forth across the river. Entire trains carrying trucks are moved across the river from the New Jersey side to Manhattan, on what look like huge rafts. Two trains per barge and two barges per crossing, with a small tug between them and a second on the starboard side. I see several such transports. They meet in the middle of the river. One has crossed our path. These tugs struggle along with their heavy loads. They rise up and almost push off from the water with their propellers, snorting and whipping the river water into the white foam behind them. The transport is very close now, inbound to New York. I count the freight cars. On the first barge there is a row of six freight cars, *box cars,* and one open car (I don't know what it's called in English), and a flatcar loaded with something that looks like large machinery beneath a green tarpaulin. The freight cars have various marks and symbols on them. Most of these are small and hard to make out, but there are a few I can read. A yellow steel boxcar with a red roof and a lot of writing on it. The big doors on the side are bright red like the roof. Next to them the name of the company is written in large red letters against the light yellow side. I read FRIGICAR. It must be a refrigerator car. The other cars are dark red. The writing on them is white. On one I can read BALTIMORE & OHIO, and on another NEW YORK CENTRAL. The open freight car is black and it, too, is made entirely of steel. There is a long name in small letters on it that I cannot quite make out, but I believe it says WESTERN MARYLAND. The other line of railroad cars on the barge seems to be only red boxcars. Seven of them. On the second barge I think I can count two rows of ten freight cars each. Here then is an entire freight train of thirty-five bogie wagons that the two small tugs pull across the river with great effort.

The MS *Kungsholm* continues up the river. Beyond the wide expressway buildings rise above one another on Manhattan. Now the road runs on iron pilings along the entire shoreline. A passenger ferry is inward bound to its berth. A large sign stands in front of the expressway, facing the water. In gigantic black letters on a white background, big enough to be seen from the other side of the river, is written:

NEW YORK CENTRAL SYSTEM

N.Y.O. & W.RY.

Squinting with my good eye, I try to make out the name of the ferry. It is written there on the wheelhouse in white letters. It's difficult to read. The ferry is old and sooty. It has red lead stains here and there. The lettering is white, after all. I think it says Catskill. There are other huge signs further inland. They have been painted directly on the fire walls of the smaller skyscrapers.

HOTEL DIXIE

HOTEL HOLLAND

The streetcars head east, right up the street we pass, and far ahead there stands the Chrysler Building. Farther down, to the right, I can see the Empire State Building, and I know that we are now on our way past the ferry berth at 42nd Street. I picture the map of Manhattan the whole time and try to identify what I am seeing. The passengers are standing next to me, talking to one another. They point towards Manhattan, calling attention to various skyscrapers, and they nudge me and want to tell me what it is I'm seeing over there. But I'm not listening. I don't want to listen to anyone. Instead, I look at the skyline and realize that I have arrived in New York.

There is still not a cloud in the sky. It's sunny and there is a light breeze. The air is clear and bright, the sky above new York is blue this fall morning, and we are now on our way in. We will be disembarking at Pier No. 97, at the foot of West 57th Street.

We are among the first ones on land. We almost always are. I don't remember that the immigration authorities even bothered to look at me. The cabin stewards had carried our luggage from the cabins, and the rest of our things were already stacked in the large customs hall. The customs agent was almost sixty. He stood there before us in the middle of the great warehouse, but did not see us. He had large tufts of white hair sticking straight out of his big red ears and his skin was pink like that of a newborn baby. He had horn-rimmed glasses, a long, dark overcoat with large folds over deep pockets, and a strange peaked cap with a high, flat crown. Gunnar walked over to him, leaned forward and said a few words. The customs agent took the documents and briefly examined them. He then saluted and motioned to the uniformed porters, who stood waiting in a group over by the wall. They were Negroes and wore red caps. Three of them came running over to carry all our baggage. One was short, with light, almost white, skin. He was old and his face wrinkled. The other two had coal-black faces, but the palms of their hands were pink. They were big and rather young. Around 25 or so. Gunnar pointed out our baggage, and the three of them loaded it up on two carts, secured it with straps and trotted off with the carts. By then Gunnar had already walked off and Alva hurried to catch up. The other passengers were now entering the customs shed. They stood in line. But I didn't see the student among them. He must still have been on board. And with this, we stepped from the customs area out into America.

Gunnar and Alva went first, then my two sisters, with the housekeeper and governess beside them, and I came. I stayed a little behind them, but not far enough to attract the attention of some customs official, policeman or other guard who might ask to see my papers, or wonder who I was and ask what I was doing, trying to pass their barriers into America.

CHAPTER 7

We are heading north in two taxicabs. These cars are American taxis and are not black like the Swedish cabs. They are yellow, with silver roof and pillars between the windows. A checkered band circles each car beneath the windows and across the hood, and on the front door there is a printed map of the United States with the words: PARMELEE SYSTEM. These cars are called Yellow Cabs. There are more of these taxis than any other kind. Gunnar and Alva and I are riding in the first one with some of the baggage. The rest of it will be delivered later. I am riding in the second cab. I sit in the backseat on the left-hand side and look out. I don't remember the others, but my sisters, the housekeeper and the governess must have been there too. That is, if the housekeeper didn't come later with the rest of the luggage. But my memory of this taxi ride is a double exposure. The first thing that comes up is a strong memory of the Hudson River. It is abnormally bright in color and simply sketched in simple lines.

We have got into the cab, closed the doors and are about to leave the pier. The driver then turns and says that he is going to take the fast way. He is wearing a brown cap and a blue tie with white dots. He has brown eyes and is unshaven. I notice his large ears. He turns off to the right, leaving the other cab, and we swing up onto the Henry Hudson Parkway. We drive along in the fast lane above the river, and in this version I remember that this is the first time I have ever been on an expressway, that the sun is glittering on the Hudson River, and that the reds and yellows of fall are already blazing in the crowns of the trees in Riverside Park. In this version we leave the expressway far uptown, around 125th street, after passing Grant's Tomb, and then drive south past the church until we reach 116th Street, where the driver makes an illegal U-turn and pulls up in front of the door of 449 Riverside Drive, where we are going to live. And now it strikes me that I have been remembering a dream, because the big, uniformed Negro doorman rushes up, opens the car door and I step out onto the red carpet beneath the canopy and up to the tall front doors. Their heavy bronze grating twists like aquatic plants in front of thick glass. With my right hand I push the revolving door that stands between the large glass doors, and it glides so smoothly that I practically have to run to avoid injuring my heels. As I stand in the high, marble foyer, the elevator boy walks towards me. He is lighter, but he too is a Negro. He opens the heavy bronze doors and they begin to carry in the baggage.

But reality should have been somewhat different. I don't think we had a real canopy, just a simple shelter from the rain, outside the door, the kind buildings generally had. The tenants could wait for their cabs there, when the weather was bad. And, in truth, I really don't remember any red carpet, either. That was the kind of thing I was to see later, outside the entrances of the buildings on Central Park West, near 63rd Street. Riverside Drive and 116th Street was still a fashionable address, but no longer the address of millionaires. And, while it was true that it was autumn in the park down by the new expressway, and the Hudson River did glitter, we had driven another way.

In a moment the memory changes, and a second, grayer memory surfaces. In this second memory of my arrival it is the noise and traffic that I remember. It is as though all Manhattan presses in with cars, buses and trucks. People yell and shout at one another, and the city is noisy. We jam ourselves into the taxicab and shut the doors. A big green truck with a load of wobbling wooden crates forces us up onto the sidewalk, just as we are about to leave the pier. The brakes screech and I have to catch myself with my hands so as not to fly forward and hit my head against the front seat. For a moment it looks as though the wooden crates will come crashing down on us, but they wobble over towards the other side and the green truck drives on. Our driver swears, rolls down the window and shakes his fist. He shouts something. Then he turns back towards me and says:

"This is about the lousiest fucking way to make a living there is."

I see the dark stubble on his cheek, his large ears and pointed chin. He hangs his elbow out the window, and he quickly looks at me with his piercing, small, brown eyes. All the way up Riverside Drive he sits muttering to himself. He drives erratically. There is a traffic light at every corner. The traffic moves sluggishly. We spend a lot of time standing still. I count the blocks. He only gets three blocks each time, before we are forced to stop and wait again. Turning on to Riverside Drive, the traffic begins to thin out. He is at the head of a large bunch of cars. The light turns red as we pull up by the road construction site at 79th Street. But he has calmed down now. He yawns. He scratches the back of his neck. When the light turns green he floors it, so he won't be passed.

I know who he is. I can read it. The name of this driver is Harry. It says so on a small notice in front of me, showing his photograph, his full name and number. It has been issued by the police department. The number of this *DRIVER* is written in extra large print.

In the photograph, he looks younger, and his face is fuller. His eyes are not as piercing. In the picture he is clean-shaven, his cap is of a light-colored material, not brown corduroy, and he is wearing a different tie. He's got on the same jacket, however, and it looks like the same shirt, although it is cleaner in the photograph.

For their own safety, passengers are supposed to write down the driver's name and number as soon as they get in the cab. Any complaints should be reported to the nearest police station or to the Hack License Bureau. His permit will expire on March 31,

1939. It is signed by the police commissioner. His name is Lewis J. Valentine. I can picture the notice before me. I remember the name Valentine because I wonder if he is related to the actor Valentino and what nationality he is. I also remember the notice because I try to figure out the meaning of Hack License Bureau. *License* is a permit and *bureau* is an office. Permit office. But I don't know what *hack* means. I have never seen the word before. Later, that afternoon, when I unpack my dictionary, I see that *hack* means 'a worn out horse.' In other words it was "The New York Police Worn-Out Horse License Bureau." It was such a funny name that I still remember the entire notice. Later, in bed, I imagined that his name was Harry Cackster and think of all he could tell me about New York. I made up a long story. It began with the truck turning over, and the crates crashing to the ground and breaking open. In the box, labelled oranges, there were really bombs. There was a gang threatening to blow up the whole city. Harry had been a childhood friend of the gang leader. The story went on and on, with one adventure after the other, the entire evening.

While we stood at the road construction site, waiting for the light to turn green, I stared at the back of Harry's neck. I had been about to mention that the porters who had carried our baggage when we disembarked were Negroes, and I had been about to say it in Swedish. I was able to stop myself in time. You weren't supposed to say that kind of thing in the presence of strangers.

"Remember never to say *neger* in Swedish," Alva had said. "It sounds like *nigger*, which is an insult. Someone might hear you and misunderstand. And you should know that in America, the word *negress* should be used neither in Swedish nor English. If you're speaking Swedish, use the word *färgad* (colored). In English you can say *colored* or *Negro*. But when you write *Negro* you must use a capital letter, just as you would with the words *French* or *German*. This is just as important as not saying *nigger* when you speak English or *neger* that sounds like *nigger* when you speak Swedish.

I looked at Harry. I could read his name, and I knew his background. But I didn't say it, because the Swedish word *neger* was not the only dangerous one. *Jude,* too, was a dangerous word. It could also be dangerous in Swedish. But in America, I was never to say the Swedish word *jude* when others were present.

"And especially not in New York, where there are so many. They will either think you are sayng *Yid,"* a disrespectful term, or else, if they have been in America a long time, they will think you are speaking German and are saying *Jude,* and that's not good. If you must say something, you can use a different term. And you should also try to avoid using the word *Jew* in English. Particularly in certain compound words. It might be misunderstood. When *Jew* is written with a small letter, it is a verb, *to jew* or *jewing,* which you must never use. You should know that when you get to New York you can be taken to court for using such a word. Use a word like *Hebrew* if you must speak of them. You must always be careful. You never know who is listening."

Actually, there were any number of dangerous words. In Swedish, we called people from Poland *polacker.* But if some Polish immigrant were to hear me use the Swedish word, he might turn around and punch me in the face because I had insulted him. The proper term was *Pole.*

You had to constantly watch your tongue. You never knew who was listening, or how they might misunderstand. It was best never to speak Swedish in America if anyone else was around. It was best to say nothing that might be taken personally. Words could have very dangerous repercussions. To think something was one thing, to say it out loud another. As long as I kept my mouth shut I could look at the back of Harry's neck and silently note that he was Jewish. You could tell by his name and appearance. My thinking this was hardly something that could offend him, since he couldn't hear anything or see it on my face and didn't know that I was thinking the word. But if I were to say it out loud, he would hear me and might fly into a rage; he might hit me or call the police.

It wasn't just here in America, or especially in New York, that it was like this. It was the same everywhere. Certain words could only be used in certain circles. You had to think hard, and try to figure out how the people you met spoke, the words and phrases they were accustomed to. Then you could drape yourself in those words and expressions and sound the same as them and that way they couldn't tell what you was thinking.

It was dangerous to repeat what I had heard at home, or to tell what I knew about people, when strangers were present. You constantly had to watch your tongue. What was said at Kvicksta could not be repeated at Äppelviken, and what Alva said should not be mentioned at Elsa's. True, they were relatives and all part of the family, but they spoke one way when they were together and another when they were in their own homes. They thought differently then. And their voices sounded different. But you were supposed to pretend not to hear it. You were supposed to pretend that there wasn't any difference between what people said to each other and what they said about each other, or between the way they spoke in one company and the way they spoke in another. There were also things you said you believed in when other people were present, and other things you really believed.

At home, with only the family around, Alva might joke about the clergy and say what she really thought about religion. But then there would be a tea party attended by some elderly, gray-haired ladies in custom-tailored suits, and some of them were church-goers, and Alva would talk of sacred music and Bach. I knew that she never listened to Bach, or to any other music, and that she was just like her father in turning off the radio when the Sunday services began, to avoid the blackcoats. She had explained it to me when I was little and my paternal grandmother had wanted me to say a prayer before going to bed.

"Don't start a discussion," she had said. "That will just make her unhappy. Pretend you are praying and she'll be happy. Then go on thinking whatever you like. You shouldn't provoke people needlessly."

It had always been like that. But you were never supposed to show that you had noticed. To eavesdrop on them was like coming upon them naked; you must never do it. At least not so that you were caught at it. You always had to watch your tongue and look as though you hadn't heard anything. There was a lot you couldn't let them know that you had ever heard. But it wasn't until we were living in the new house in Äppelviken, in the spring of 1938, that I really overheard very much. The house had been designed so that my parents' suite would form a completely separate upper storey with two bedrooms, a private bath, a study and a sitting-room alcove, and a fireplace, filing area, library, spacious terrace, and two exits, straight onto the garden or the street. A stairway led from this free-standing upper floor down to the lower level. The lower floor also had doors leading to the street and the garden. Downstairs, the focal point was a multi-purpose room, which was generally occupied by the children and servants, except when it was used for dining.

The house had been designed to take advantage of the natural slope of the ground, and to provide each floor with several functions. On our floor, facing the garden there was the upper cellar and storeroom, then the housekeeper's room, the kitchen and pantry. Towards Nyängsvägen, there was the garage, the bathroom for servants and children, the governess's bedroom connecting with the nursery and, in the far corner, a sleeping cubicle for me. The nursery had been designed so that in the future it could be split into similar sleeping cubicles. A new doorway could then be opened out into the multi-purpose room. That way there would be one bedroom and three sleeping cubicles in a row. When the children had moved out, assistants and overnight guests could sleep there. The sleeping cubicles were not real rooms. Markelius had designed them together with Alva. They represented an innovation in the concept of housing. During the day the children would play outside or collectively in the multi-purpose room. The cubicles were intended only to be slept in; they held precisely the volume of air necessary for healthy sleep. To provide this air, they were ventilated with specially constructed windows.

My cubicle was furnished with an eye to the utiliatarian. When you pushed open the thick door (soundproofed with a gray felt pad in the middle), it opened with a slam like a refrigerator, since it lacked both lock and handle. It was held in place by a spring mechanism. Entering, the bed was to the left. There was just enough room for the door. The bed was meant to be folded into the wall during the day. There were special straps to hold the bedding in place. The wall back there was only a varnished sheet of plywood, with the nursery's double closet on the other side. Against the whitewashed outer wall to the right, 28 feet in, stood a black bookshelf, with eight 32-foot shelves. Directly below the window stood a square black table, with a yellow plywood table-top. There was a black chair by the table. Behind the chair there stood a 32 foot wide closet, whose sliding doors were hidden in the wall. With the bed down, you could just slip between the bookshelf and the bed, past the corner of the bed to the chair between the closet doors and the table. I had no curtains. Curtains were old-fashioned. They collected dust. Instead, there were adjustable yellow wooden blinds built into he window. But outside my window on Nyängsvägen, there was a street lamp. At night, the light shone right in on me through the blinds, because the bed was placed so that my head was toward the wall of the multi-purpose room. But if I turned around, with my head toward the sheet of plywood, and lay on my left side, the light no longer bothered me and I could sleep.

There were several ingenious ways to keep a window open and let air into a room. Bu it was more difficult to get a window to shut tightly. So, when it was windy outside, the draft made a whistling noise. And just below the window, there was a narrow vent that you could adjust with a small brass-knobbed screw. It could not be shut entirely, however, because of the need for ventilation. There was always a draft on my left shoulder when I did my homework at the table. The window had a new kind of sill, a thin sheet of synthetic gray material. It was thin and brittle. I broke off the corner nearest the closet, fell backwards and hit my head against the edge of the table the day we moved in, when I had stepped on it to reach the upper cupboard, where I wanted to hide some magazines. But no one noticed. The floor was covered in some gray substance, and to make it easier to swab off, it sloped up a decimeter towards the outer walls. Rubber heels made ugly scuff marks on the floor, so you weren't allowed to wear shoes in the room. From the ceiling there hung a large globe of frosted white glass that spread a shadowless light. In spring 1938 there were no paintings or pictures on the wall and I had been given black metal angle irons to keep my books in place. It wasn't good for the book covers to stand without support.

I supplemented my weekly allowance by pasting newspaper clippings about Alva and Gunnar on thick yellow paper in big black binders. They would eventually be placed in an archive, so it was especially important that I do a good job. I sat in their study at Gunnar's large desk. His desk was always the least cluttered, and therefore the best place to work. The light shone down on me from the skylight, and I was very careful, cutting with the large paper scissors and pasting so that everything looked straight and the margins came out nice and even. I had to read while I pasted, so as not to cut at the wrong spot or glue so the article didn't make sense. It was easy enough to lose the end of an article if I was careless and forgot to read it. One of the things I read in these clippings was how modern and progressive our house was. In the future, everyone would live like this. But there were also many articles poking fun at the house. They mentioned the round bathroom window that looked like a porthole, and Alva and Gunnar's part of the house with its sliding panel walls, skylights and teak railings off the sleeping cabin facing Nyängsvägen. They said that the house looked like a steamboat. Actually, it did, but they needn't have joked about it. It might have been thought stylish.

I always defended the house when people talked to me about it. I told them how functional it was. It was completely different from the ordinary houses my classmates lived in. Our house looked like one of the ones featured in the big picture books on houses in France and Germany, the kind that had been on display at the Stockholm Exhibition. It was also fun to look at the blueprints. And I didn't let on that the flat roof leaked, the way people said flat roofs always did in Sweden, where there was so much rain and snow.

"No," I said, "it doesn't leak. Flat roofs are good and functional."

Every time someone began to talk about the house when I was away from home, I was always prepared to defend it. Everyone laughed at it. They all lived in regular, old-fashioned houses.

Almost the entire roof covering the lower floor also served as a large terrace for the second storey, where Gunnar and Alva lived. Markelius had put a lot of thought into this terrace. I was special. There was to be a real sandy beach with a shower. It was made so you could put up special screens, lie there naked sunning yourself like at the beach, and then go shower off the sand. But for some reason, the drainage never worked properly, even though it was especially constructed, and we couldn't have sand up there after the first time. Nor could you lie naked. Gunnar tried it once, but a neighbor up the hill phoned the police. Gunnar maintained that the neighbor must have climbed up on the roof to see onto the terrace.

"The dirty old man!" Gunnar had said.

The multi-purpose room, also known as the family room, was used for large dinner parties and could be partitioned with drapes, depending on the size of the party. The southern wall, towards Bävervägen and Stora Mossen, was one big bay window, which became a winter garden where the plants screened the view from the street. The other walls were whitewashed, like in a museum, to provide the paintings with a tranquil background. A large green carpet, which Alva called "the green meadow," covered the oak parquet floor.

When the guests first arrived, they went into the lower hall, with the large closet for outdoor clothes and bathroom used by servants, children and guests. If it was a large or medium-sized dinner party, they then gathered for drinks on the big green carpet by the bay window, in the multi-purpose room. Alva and Gunnar liked to offer their guests a martini, shaken by Gunnar himself, as was the custom in America. The liquor cabinet of polished light birch, with its numerous mirrors that could be opened, was upstairs next to the big blue sofa, which had been displayed at the Stockholm Exhibition. Guests gathered up there for drinks with olives and hor d' oeuvres, if it was an intimate dinner party for six or eight people.

As the guests gathered, final preparations were being made in the kitchen. The tables were concealed behind the heavy white drapes that ran in a track across the ceiling. They looked like wavy white walls, and looped around different ways, depending on whether it was a small dinner, a regular-sized dinner for twelve, or a large dinner party, with tables set at right angles to each other. The house had been designed for dinner parties with up to thirty guests. Seating arrangements were indicated on a red leather chart, which stood on the black table in the hall. Many guests would return to it again and again, so as not to forget where, and with whom, they were sitting. When dinner was about to be served, Alva would clap her hands and sing out, the heavy satin drapes were parted and each gentleman took his lady and escorted her to her seat.

The table had been custom-made by Svenskt Tenn to go with the house. Three tables could be joined together. The main table, the one used if there were no more than twelve guests, which always stood in the large dining alcove, was the finest. It had black legs, black edging, and a beautiful, retractable, golden-yellow leaf of polished birch. At this table, the guests were served without a tablecloth, on placemats, since the top was considered a work of art. When especially many guests came they used the table in the nursery and the one where I usually did my homework. They were ours only for everyday use. But since they didn't have such beautiful tops, they were covered in large, shiny, yellow tablecloths. And because of this the setting was different. They had tried to get me to go around, offering the guests hors d'oeurvres from a small tray. But I ate some of what I was supposed to be serving, had my tie on wrong, and spilled, and they only asked me to do that once.

Since the door out to the multi-purpose room was sound-proofed, I could only hear a low murmur in my room from these dinner parties. I had already eaten. The only problem was that I couldn't go out to piss because I would have to pass through the multi-purpose room and all the guests. But when there was a party out there, I had a little potty I could use if I needed it. I never overheard any of the conversation or saw who visited the house, since I was already in my room when the guests began to arrive at seven-thirty.

Nonetheless, I heard a great deal that spring. And Markelius was responsible. In designing the house, with an independent upper storey and a lower storey shifted off center in relation to the one above, and with a stairwell that wound down from above, opening out into the spacious multi-purpose room, he had created a old-fashioned phonograph cone. And the thing Alva and Gunnar never knew (and never could themselves hear, since no one else was allowed up there, so that the upper storey was always silent when they were downstairs) was that every word spoken up there echoed down into the hall. It was only when they went into the bedroom, closing all the doors behind them, that their voices faded into a low murmur. Everything else they said to each other, thinking themselves alone up there, echoed down to us. The acoustics were remarkable. If I stood right up against the wall, just where the hall became the multi-purpose room, I could hear every whisper from up there as if they were standing behind me whispering confidences into my ear.

After the dinner parties that spring in the new house, as I lay awake and heard the last guests depart, I used to sneak into the kitchen after the lights went out and take some of the leftover dessert. I could hear them talking up there.

It was then I heard what they were really thinking. They talked about the guests. They told each other what this one had said and what that one had done. They talked about how their guests had looked and what they had worn. They walked the floor up there, back and forth, and talked to each other. Sometimes they sat down for a moment. Sometimes it fell silent, when one of them went into the bathroom and shut the door. Otherwise, their voices echoed down in the big megaphone. They didn't limit themselves to commenting on the appearance and words of their guests, they judged them and drew conclusions:

"He's become so strangely unsure of himself," said Alva.

"Senility," said Gunnar.

"I don't think so," Alva said. "It's more like he's lost his intellectual footing with this last divorce. When he was thanking me for dinner, he got entangled in childhood memories from Strindberg's Dalarö, although he actually meant Kymmendö. Later, during the discussion about Borgese, he had nothing to contribute. It was as though he hadn't kept up with the debate on *Goliath*. He didn't say one thing worth remembering the entire evening. He's not usually like that. He just sat watching her all evening, worrying about what she might do."

"This is the first time he has shown her off in public," said Gunnar. "It takes a lot of energy to keep an eye on her. Obviously, he doesn't have time to get much reading done. Borgese he hadn't read, in any case."

"Did you notice that he's begun to cut the hair around his temples short, so as not to show that he is turning gray? She's younger than both of his daughters."

Alva laughed a little as she said this and the sound of ice clinking against glass could be heard.

"Yes," said Gunnar a moment later. "It shows in the way he dresses. He looks so youthful now. What's more, he's changed his manner. He giggles all the time now. He even does it in the middle of meetings. The question is just whether he got hold of her because he noticed that he was losing his short-term memory and becoming giggly, or whether he began to suffer from presenility before he remarried."

"In any case, she is vulgar, isn't she?" said Alva. "Didn't you notice how low-cut her dress was? She really went around sticking them out. She was already buzzed during cocktails too. And then she flirted with all the men, and sat on their laps, one after the other. And he just sat there looking miserable and drinking too much again."

"But she is some peach," said Gunnar. "And just twenty-two. She sure knows how to get the attention of the men, looking so cute, her mouth open, when you talk to her. She tilts her head, opens her eyes wide, and opens and closes her mouth like a fish out of water. I suppose that's the way she got through school. There are girls like that."

"Yes, but he doesn't have to marry them," said Alva.

"There aren't that chances left anymore for him," commented Gunnar. "This third marriage is his last chance. He's only got two more years before retirement. He intends to use them to keep her under control at least."

"I couldn't help looking at her when you quoted Borgese on Mussolini's policies," Alva said with a laugh. "It is in the rulers' interest that their subjects are indigent in spirit."

"That was Plato," said Gunnar. "And Mussolini is more of a man, in any case."

I gathered that they were talking about an old professor who had married a young university student. When we lived in the Tham house in Olovslund, he used to visit on Sunday afternoon, with a gray-haired lady, his second wife. They wore matching tweed suits, hers with a skirt and his with knickerbockers. They had been on their Sunday walk on Ekerö, around Drottningholm. On their way home they had walked through Nockeby so they could stop in at the Myrdals' for a cup of coffee and a visit, he said when he phoned to invite himself over. They used to take the Number 12 streetcar into town, when they left in the evening. It had been a while since I had seen him now.

I listened only a short time down there, at the end of the great funnel. It wasn't particularly interesting this time. I went into the kitchen and opened the refrigerator door. The guests had eaten Parisian flan on a bed of apricots. There was half a cake left. I got out a saucer and made a cut straight across the cake, so it wouldn't be apparent that I had taken any. There was also some cream left over. On the way back to bed, I stopped to hear if they had changed the subject. But now they were just talking about Mussolini. They had given the dinner party to discuss a book about Mussolini which had just been published in America. Alva said something about Freud and mass psychology, and said that Mussolini was living proof of Le Bon's law on the spiritual unity of the masses.

"He is master of the mass-soul."

"When I get to be sixty, you'll have to get me one of those cute little peaches," said Gunnar. "Promise me you will!"

They certainly didn't talk like that when they knew that I was around. This was their way of speaking when they were alone. There were different ways of talking for different occasions. The important thing was that no one heard one's own private thoughts, and that no one realized you had overheard. They caught me just once, and it was a time I hadn't even intended to listen.

I had come up to Alva and Gunnar's study to get some paper in April. The door to the upper hallway was open and as I was about to enter I heard them talking. I stopped in the doorway and looked at them. They didn't see me where I was standing. But when I heard what they were saying, I realized that I had made a mistake. I stopped in my tracks. Now I couldn't just start walking into the room without them thinking I had been standing there eavesdropping. If, on the other hand, I took a step backwards and tried to go down the stairs, they would hear and see me. And that would be just as unfortunate. So I stood there without moving and pretended that I wasn't there and no one could see me. Instead, I listened as they sat facing each other discussing their friends. The sun was out and it shone through the skylight and down on the beautiful desk of polished birch. The books and manuscripts were stacked neatly. Alva had taken out the typewriter, but had swiveled her chair toward Gunnar and Gunnar had put his fountain pen down.

They had given a large dinner party the night before. From time to time Alva laughed. They didn't see me and spoke as they usually did when they were alone. But this time they weren't talking about Freud or Mussolini at all, only about their guests. They had talked about one of them present at the party, who had pretended to kill himself to be rid of his mistress, and how a second had failed in his ambition to become a professor and instead was the father of some third guest's child, and about the guest who had left the party early, claiming that he had so much work to do that he had to return to the ministry in the middle of the night, that he was an old pederast, and that his wife, who was really only his wife for appearance's sake, had swindled the insurance company after their house burned down and had received a lot more money than was coming to her. Alva had chattered and laughed, and Gunnar had drunk cherry brandy from his little silver cup. And they had had a great time, occasionally interrupting each other. Then, all of a sudden, they had noticed me. Gunnar saw me first. His face froze and he stopped talking in the middle of a sentence. Alva turned and saw me standing in the doorway. Then she said something in French. They had stopped talking English to each other when I was around the previous winter because I was studying English now and could understand them.

Gunnar was the first to speak to me.

"Don't stand there evesdropping!"

"I didn't mean to overhear what you were saying. I just came to get some paper."

But I knew they didn't believe me.

"Only scoundrels eavesdrop," said Gunnar.

"But *darling,*" Alva said to Gunnar, "perhaps he didn't mean to."

"You must never tell anyone anything you hear at home," she said to me. "Do you understand?"

"I don't say anything," I said.

"I know we can count on you," she said smiling.

"I didn't want to listen," I said.

"You're no eavesdropper," she said. "We know that."

And I thought to myself: now her voice has gone twittery

again. Gunnar just stared at me. I stood perfectly still. There was nothing I could do or say.

"People might misunderstand," she went on. "You know how people are. They just don't understand. They might think we are gossiping. But we're just interested in human nature."

Now Gunnar said something to her in French. She shook her head, and turning back to me, said:

"We have to discuss things that others don't talk about, you see. It's important for us to understand how people behave, to know what people are really like. We have to know that in order to be able to form an opinion of them. But other people might misunderstand if they hear about it. It would just cause trouble. Others wouldn't understand. They aren't able to see themselves objectively, they lack insight. Most people dislike hearing that they are being talked about. So one should never discuss people except when one is alone. We were wrong not to have shut the door. But you mustn't take advantage of our mistake and tell what you've heard. What you hear at home, you must never repeat to anyone. Not even our relatives. Promise me!"

"I promise," I said. "Can I have the paper now?"

Alva took out a thick sheaf of typing paper (there must have been 150 pieces) and gave them to me. She also gave me ten pieces of carbon paper, without my having asked. Gunnar just sat there, silent, his lips pressed tightly together, looking at me. I shut the door properly as I left and stomped down the stairs, so that they would hear that I wasn't standing by the door evesdropping.

I looked at Harry's neck in front of me. He had a pimple there, just below his left ear. He didn't know what I was thinking. I would never, never let anyone hear what I was thinking. We were crossing 116th street and were almost there. The trees in the park were already turning yellow and red and beyond was the river. The doorman and elevator boy were carrying our luggage into 449 Riverside Drive, our new American Address.

CHAPTER 8

Our apartment is on the eleventh floor. The elevator is roomy. The mirrors and mahogany make it shine and there is a red plush sofa against the back wall of the elevator. A brass sign reads Otis Brothers. The elevator boy wears a red uniform jacket with brass buttons. He operates the elevator with the same type of lever used by the streetcar drivers. He is good at it. He stops on the dot and opens the grating when the car reaches the eleventh floor. The landing is small, the walls covered in marble. The stairway is straight ahead. The black iron railing at the stairwell is twisted in a vine pattern. Where the stairs reach the landing, and where the next flight of stairs, leading to the roof, begin, the railings end at six-foot, black, hexagonal, iron columns. At the top of each column is a newly-polished, gleaming brass sphere the size of a child's head. If I walk to the railing between the columns I can see all the way down the stairwell to the reception desk eleven floors below. Voices can be heard from there.

Looking down the stairs, I can see that there, too, the railing ends at a black iron column, again with a large, gleaming brass sphere on top. Behind it, on the landing between floors, there is a French window with a protective wrought-iron grating with an aquatic-plant pattern. There is also a false balcony, with the same black wrought-iron grating serving as a railing outside. You can see the white droppings of the pigeons on the window pane. Through the grating and glass, the river can be seen. When I look up the stairway, I notice that there, too, the railing to the landing half-way up ends in a black iron column crowned with a gleaming brass sphere. Through the window the sky and pigeons are visible. They fly over and perch on the little false balcony, where they hunt for lice in their feathers. I hear them cooing.

Where I step out of the elevator here on the eleventh floor, our black door is to the right. Opening it, I stand in the hall and cloakroom. To the left, in the corner, there is a brass umbrella stand and a telephone on a low black table. That telephone connects us to the doorman eleven floors below. He uses it to tell us that we have visitors and to ask if they are welcome. It is also used by guests when they want him to call them a cab. Straight ahead, behind closed sliding doors, is the closet for outdoor clothes. The ceiling is high. I'm almost sure there is a picture in a small gold frame hanging over the telephone, but I can't see it in my mind. I do know that it's behind glass.

There are three doors off the hall. All the doors in the apartment are white and have notched brass doorknobs that turn, instead of the door handles I am accustomed to. There are no sills between the rooms. To the left there is a double door leading to our large living room. The left half is bolted at the floor and ceiling. Opening the other half, I can see into the room. In front of me, there is a balcony and four large windows facing the river. The balcony is on the far left. There are the same type of French windows as on the landings between floors. This isn't a real balcony either. Just a ledge with a railing along the cornice, running the length of the façade. Below the four windows sit exceptionally large white radiators, with big brass knobs. If you touch the radiators when the heat is on, you burn yourself. They are hot and filled with steam.

This is a spacious room. All the furniture is American because we have rented a furnished apartment. There is a coal fire burning in the fireplace, but it's not really burning. It's merely a device, an electric heater hidden in something made to look like glowing coals. On a large white rug in front of the artificial fire stands a long, low coffee table with brass legs and a thick slab of glass for a top. On either side of the table there are swelling yellow sofas. Each sofa can accomodate three people. They have loose puffy cushions. A green bowl with a bunch of purple grapes sits on the glass table. The grapes are made of glass. Next to it stands an austere white vase that generally holds a single tulip sticking up through the neck, as well as a large round brass ashtray. Further into the room, to the left, there is a solitary, well stuffed green armchair and footstool. This is a reading chair. Beside it stands a floor lamp with a pink fabric shade. The footstool is on a round white rug with a blue border. In the window behind the armchair there is a Kentia palm; its large blue and white porcelain pot is hidden

At the far wall, to the left and in front of the balcony, stands a mahogany desk. There is a real phone on the desk, one you can use for outside calls or just to reach the second phone in the master bedroom. Next to the phone, there is an inkstand, a leather writing pad, a large ashtray, and *The American College Dictionary*. Behind them, against the wall, is a low white bookshelf. There ought to be a picture hanging on the wall above it; there's a place for one. But I don't see it. I don't see any pictures at all, hanging in this living room.

If I take a couple more steps into the room and turn to the right, I can see a second stuffed green armchair and footstool on another round, white rug. The border of this rug is red. This armchair, too, is flanked by a floor lamp with a pink fabric shade. But here there is also a small table. It is a round, beaten-brass tabletop on curved, black legs. It stands against the white wall next to the door leading into the hallway. Further on, I can see into the dining room. There is no door between living room and dining room. Rather, there is an arched opening with a blue curtain, which can be dropped into place. The curtain is held back on the right by a brass chain attached to a hook in the wall. When it is unhooked, the entire curtain falls and covers the passageway into the dining room. But now the curtain is gathered together and chained in place. The dining room has a window on the courtyard. When you look out this window you can see the bathroom window behind the master bedroom. But there is frosted glass in the bathroom window, so you can't see inside. Next to the window there is a door leading into the pantry. This door cannot be locked, it has double hinges and can be pushed open from either side. There is a small pane of glass at eye-level, so you don't bump into someone else when pushing it open, and so that the servants can see how far dinner has progressed. In the middle of the room there is a big, brown oval table, with twelve chairs around it. To the right stands a large brown sideboard. On it are silver salt and pepper shakers, a glass jar of mustard and two glass cruets, one for oil and one for vinegar. On the wall to my left hang six large blue-and-white plates that look Dutch. They show windmills and girls in wooden shoes. A brass chandelier with six light bulbs can be seen over the table. A silk cord with a tassel hangs from it. When you pull the cord a bell rings in the kitchen and the number board by the pantry door indicates that the call is from number tow. There is space for twelve numbers on the board, but only six are used.

Off the hall, to the right, there are two doors. The smaller one is to the guest bathroom. The larger door opens into the corridor leading into the apartment. When I open this door, I see three glowing light bulbs near the ceiling. They hang there in a row from their brown cords, softened only by small lampshades of milk-white glass. On the right side of the corridor there is storage space. On the left, the first door is to the kitchen, then the door to the housekeeper's room, then the door to the servants' bathroom, then the door to the nurse's room. Then a small corridor goes to the left and another to the right and my room is straight ahead. The corridor to the left leads to the master bedroom. It has its own bathroom inside the room. The corridor on the right leads to the children's bathroom and my sisters' room. My sisters have a corner room with windows facing both east and south.

My room is large. it is almost four times as big as my cubicle in Äppelviken. There is room for two tables and two bookshelves, two regular chairs and an easy chair in addition to a bed. And I can still sprawl out on the floor and read, if I want.

Through my window I can see the big building across the street. At night the lights shine in there. The façade looks like a huge illuminated advertisement. The lights in the windows go on and off. If the curtains aren't drawn, I can see into the apartments with my strong eye. Most of the rooms I see are kitchens, but there are also living rooms, and even bedrooms, where people are visible at night. I can stand in the dark in my room and there, on the far side of the courtyard, people move around in perfect silence behind their windows. They open doors and walk into rooms on the other side of the windows and from my invisible vantage point I imagine their apartments behind those stage doors. If I look with my other eye, my special eye, it is all a spectacle of glitter and color, and I can fantasize about them. They open the door and I switch eyes, transform their images, as they become indistinct. During the day the façade is gray and lifeless, the windows dull and dark. Then I can see into the courtyard and over the rooftop of the other building to the east. But in the evening, with the sun setting behind me, the windows suddenly gleam opaquely like tinfoil. Then darkness comes suddenly and all at once everything inside becomes visible.

Beneath the window, the radiator vibrates from the heat. There are long brown curtains hanging at the windows. They run on yellow wooden rings on a brown curtain rod and the fringes reach all the way to the floor. When I draw the curtains during the day, it is almost pitch black in the room. In the evening, with the curtains drawn, no one can see in. Knowing just how much can be seen, I always draw my curtains before switching on the lights.

There are closets on either side of the door and above the door is a cupboard. I have a door opening on the corridor and another door level with the closet. Between the outer and inner doors is something that resembles a small compartment. When the doors are open, I can see down to the end of the corridor. But I can also shut the doors. There are locks on both doors, and for the first time in my life I can lock myself in. No one can hear what I'm doing through these two doors, and no one can come into my room without my permission. Here, at the far eastern end of the corridor, in the northern apartment on the eleventh floor, at 449 Riverside Drive, near 116th street, on the island of Manhattan's Hudson River shore, in New York City, U.S.A., in the Western Hemisphere, on the planet Earth, in the Universe, here I finally get my very own room where I can lock myself in and be myself.

CHAPTER 9

I am standing in the living room looking out at the river my first night in the New World. There is no longer a steady stream of cars down on the expressway. Solitary vehicles light up the roadway with their headlights. They sweep by down below, one by one. The bridge up there is a glittering ribbon, across the river, and I can see a ferry inward bound to West 125th Street, even though it is late. The neon sign on the far side of the river changes and says: THE TIME IS NOW 3:45 AM. The night is clear; it seems to me as if there is a full or almost full moon, and the waters of the Hudson gleam white, like a band of silver; clouds sweep swiftly across the sky; raggedy black clouds chase by, occasionally obscuring the moon. But the image I remember is almost too distinct. It is like the wood engravings in the old Harper's Weekly from the 1870s that I would browse through the following year, while waiting to be called into the doctor's office for my shots. But now it is early Sunday morning, September 11, 1938, and I stand by the window looking west onto the river.

I have been dreaming. But it isn't because of the dream that I got up. I awoke and got up out of curiosity. I wanted to see the river at night. I still remembered the dream. I stood there remembering; but although it was dramatic, it wasn't particularly frightening. Actually, it was several dreams. When I thought about them, they separated. They surfaced several abreast. I was to blame for the ferry that went down. The people in the water. The eyes. The gaping mouths. The screams drowned out by the roar of cranes. We were on our way in when the ferry exploded just off the Battery. It floated toward shore belly up and the bombs tumbled out of the hold. Then came the violent explosion. Actually, the ferry had been lying at berth, and the dream begins as each object

is found. Then it explodes. The boat also goes under. The storm
seizes it, and the waves lift and finally crush it. All that's left is
splinters. How many perished? It hadn't been decided here, but in
Washington, in the White House. And yet, the dream had actually
been quite different. It was in Germany, or rather Old Russia,
because the priests wore long beards, and I had known the
pogroms were about to take place. "Take the gold," I had said.
But I hadn't told them what I had seen. That was before they
were dragged from their cottages. Perhaps it had something to do
with the boy who had eaten the apple and fallen ill, whom the
police seized when he returned to Germany. But the ferry exploded before it made it across Upper Bay. And yet, none of this is
frightening. These were dreams played against a white wall and I
could make them go away. I had got up out of curiosity.

It's light on the other shore. Below me, in the street, several
cars, five, approach, one after the other. The river never rests. If I
were standing on the bank, I would be able to hear the sound of
the water. Now I see a harbor tug sailing up the river toward me.
Looking downstream, I see other tugs crossing the river with
barges. They work through the night. The neon sign changes
again: THE TIME IS NOW 4:05 AM. By the way, New York is an
old city. It's older than Saint Petersburg, later known as Petrograd
and then Leningrad. I yawn. I feel sleepy again. I turn, go back
through the living room, along the corridor and into my room.
Once there, I shut the door. In bed again, the covers pulled over
me and my pillow punched so it's just right under my neck, I start
to laugh to myself at the thought of what Emil Norlander wrote
about kindness to animals. Dropping a cat out the window to save
it the trouble of walking down the stairs can hardly be considered
kindness to animals; to stroke the snout of a crocodile would be
impractical; the boy who petted the brewer's horse had to learn to
write with his left hand and the man who stuck his head into the
doghouse to say hello to the bulldog lost not only his hair but the

whole works. And the illustration shows the dog running off with the man's bleeding fingers, the boy painting the fence with the poodle; the woman is petting the crocokile's snout, its jaws agape; she grins and the cat arches its back. I like Emil Norlander. I bought the book myself in August at Björk and Börjeson on Drottninggatan in Stockholm. The name Jan Myrdal 1938 appears in a sprawling script on the flyleaf. It is one of the books I have brought with me to America. I read it that evening, while sitting in the bathtub. Since I bought the book with my own money, no one can forbid me to read it in the tub. Still, Gunnar would scold me, if he caught me reading there.

It really doesn't matter if my own books get a bit wet. The pages curl a little, that's all. I like to read in the tub. When I do, I lock the door, so that no one will walk in. I lean my head against a headrest that looks like a belt stretched across the bathtub, and I hold the book up and read and giggle and laugh out loud. But I let the water run, so that no one will hear me giggling and laughing, so that no one will bang on the door, shout and wonder what I am doing. The title of Emil Norlander's book is *Sådan är du* (That's the Way You Are). It's one of my favorite bathtub books. The water gushes out, the steam fills the bathroom like a sauna, now that the hot water faucet is open. The hot water gurgles and Emil Norlander writes so vividly that you can picture the words as you read them, and I laugh amidst the roar of the water till I almost choke.

"Yes, I fear that a loving couple could sit down on a park bench in late May and not get up again before the attendants arrive at the end of October to put the bench back in the storeroom for the winter. They would thus fall totally out of step with the rest of the world, and with the stars in their eyes completely forget that there ever was such a thing as fried porridge."

The book had cost me a mere fifty öre. I had walked by Björk and Börjeson on my way to Tegelbacken, to catch the Number 12 home. I stopped to look in the shop window. Then I opened the door and went in. I could only afford books on the low-price counter, with its detective stories and such; and there lay Emil Norlander's book, right in the middle of the trash. It had a hard binding; its covers were marbled. When I picked it up and held it in my hand, it fell open to the page where he describes what it is like to make a telephone call.

"The caller can no longer speak clearly. With both feet he stands treading on the upside-down desk drawer. He's shoved one of his fists two feet into the foundation wall, where the phone has been installed, while he scratches his head with the other."

There was a picture of this, too. The inkwell had tipped over and the ink splashed. The man stamped his right foot with his mouth wide open and you could see that he was shouting. He had struck the telephone with his fist, so that it flew off the wall and smashed to pieces. A chair was tipped over. I burst out laughing right there in the shop. I just had to have that book.

It was Gunnar who first got me to go to Björk and Börjeson's well-stocked antiquarian bookstore. One day in March he had suddenly walked into my cubicle when I was sick in bed. I had been in bed almost a week. I had a bronchial infection high up in my chest. That was the diagnosis of Rolf Bergman one fall, when I was ill and they asked him what was wrong with me. I used to be bothered with a bronchial infection for a week, now and then, especially in the fall and spring. Now I was no longer so feverish. Suddenly, that afternoon, Gunnar opened the door.

"I heard you were sick," he said. "Try to get well. In any case, you should put the time to good use."

He held a package in his hand. He put it down on the bed. It was a package of books in green wrapping paper.

"When I heard you were sick I went by Björk and Börjeson and got you something to read," he said. "You should make it a habit to go there. You should use your allowance sensibly. Some of their books are inexpensive. After all, you are ten now."

"I'll be eleven in July," I said.

"Yes, now that you're ten, you can read real books," he said. "Don't forget the words of Ecclesiastes 10:18. 'Through idleness of the hands the house droppeth through.' Take the opportunity to read while you're sick and can't go to school. You must learn to use your time wisely. Get well now."

When he had gone back upstairs, I opened the package. It contained several books. There was a stack of uncut booklets, six in a series entitled *Great Men of Distinction*. They dealt with Francis of Assisi, Carlyle, Darwin, Linnaeus, Dante and Socrates. Their covers were soiled and torn. They were bound together with a string. I noticed that the lot of them had cost one and a half crowns.

There were two volumes of Kropotkin's collected works. They were entitled *The French Revolution 1789-1793*. They, too, were uncut. They had cost three crowns.

There was also a volume of Voltaire, *Philosophical Novels*. The pages of this book had not only been cut, the entire back cover was missing. It had cost 1.75.

I read the Voltaire that same afternoon. He wrote well. I skipped the preface and that sort of thing. There were parts that were slower than others, but I liked the parts about the oyster that spoke with Pythagoras and the men who defecated in their hats and a lot more.

I spent a long time with *The French Revolution*. It was a book that required a lot of thought. The past winter I had read about that revolution mainly from the Napoleonic point of view. Bonaparte fascinated me, despite the fact that he had been a dictator and that Mussolini, who was also Italian, claimed to be a new Napoleon. I told myself that there was a difference between the two, that one could both like Napoleon and dislike Mussolini.

I had three books about Napoleon. Gunnar must have given

them to me for Christmas. I hadn't bought them myself, and no one else would have given me that kind of book. One of the books was written by a German. It was missing both covers. It's style was rather frumpish. It began with the nursing infant and ended with insistent reminders that the man was a warning and a bad example for the youth of Europe. There was also a lot about kissing and romance, about how Napoleon missed his wife and such. I quickly read through it and put it aside.

The second book was big and thick. To be sure, it was only paper-bound, but the cover was pretty, with silver print on down green paper. Napoleon's imperial coat-of-arms was printed on it. You could feel the crest with your fingertips. This book was in French, so I couldn't read it, but that didn't matter too much, since it included more than 1000 illustrations. Several of these were in color. I like the first one best. It was entitled *Napoleon at Arcole*. It depicted the incident at Arcole, when Napoleon, in order to dispel the discouragement and reluctance of his soldiers, grabs the French tricolor and himself leads his grenadiers across the bridge. It was then that Napoleon became convinced that his will could conquer the world and that he was destined for great things and invulnerable, a new Alexander, a 26-year-old general who had rejected the lackadaisical and indecisive warfare of the time, and who, thanks to a rare combination of cold reason and fervent imagination, was able to throw the full weight of his forces swiftly and decisively on the enemy's most vulnerable spot, to crush his scattered opponents in battle after battle and to take the war deep into enemy territory. The locks of his hair fly in the breeze; his gaze is steady, the set of his mouth both sensitive and determined. Here then is the young hero who has captured the attention of all Europe. In this color picture, young Bonaparte glances back to his grenadiers, looking them in the eye, to inspire them to follow him to victory. And that's just the way I wished I looked. But I didn't. The picture of Napoleon on horseback crossing the Alps was another of my favorites. But it wasn't as good as the other one.

The third book was the one I returned to again and again. It wasn't about love or that kind of thing, but about revolution and war, about how Emperor Napoleon finally died of stomach cancer without proper medical care, a prisoner on the rocky island Saint Helena in the Atlantic, watched over by a small-minded prison warden. I can see this book clearly in my mind. I can see the old-fashioned Swedish spelling of the words. And I can hear long passages from the book, hear them written in the old way. This book also had pictures. There was the same picture of Bonaparte at Arcole, but here it was smaller and in black and white. But although I can see the picture and clearly recall the appearance of the text, and though I can feel the cover beneath my fingers, I am unable to retrieve the name of the author from my memory.

But Kropotkin's name is not lost. He introduced me to the French Revolution and made me abandon Bonaparte in March 1938. Nevertheless, I couldn't help admiring him. Kropotkin also made me read Dickens' *Tale of Two Cities* from a different viewpoint. He made me see the Mountain's betrayal and Robespierre's vacillation, how he didn't dare carry the revolution through to completion, but instead struck the golden mean and thus paved the way for the reactionary triumph of the 9th Thermidor and for Napoleon Bonaparte's coup d'état of the 18th Brumaire, which resulted in dictatorship and the empire. It was that spring, while reading Kropotkin, that I truly realized I belonged with the people in their struggle against the forces of order. It was right to send Louis XVI to the scaffold. I myself would have been one of the majority voting for the unconditional death sentence.

"Citizens," said Jan Myrdal (tall and dark, with flashing eyes and metallic voice) addressing the Convention following the interrogation of the royal arch-traitor.

It was as if a tremor briefly shook the entire assembly when I stood up. They were electrified. A buzzing passed through the chamber as all eyes turned to the young speaker, known justifiably out in the sections as the Nation's Conscience.

"Citizens, Frenchmen! How is it possible that a person can be so vile, so consummately mendacious, as this Louis, who has addressed us? Yes, it is the royal traditions, the influence of the Jesuits and other blackcoats, which has convinced this individual that anything is permitted a king. France's peasants, who have refused to pay the feudal charges, who have driven off the nobles, done away with feudal rights, seized their land, opposed the clergy, apprehended the émigrés despite their disguises and captured the fleeing Louis, the French peasants demand that we patriots do our duty. Long live the sansculottes! Death to the royal traitor!"

All the republicans in the chamber around me now broke into a chant, "Death! Death!" and the despicable Girondists shrank together in fear, trying to slink away.

For me, then, Bonaparte was succeeded by the revolution.

Francis of Assisi, on the other hand, did not interest me, and so I put aside the booklets on the men of distinction. To be sure, I planned to read the one about Darwin, but by the time I had finished Kropotkin, I was no longer sick and had to go back to school; later, I never got around to it.

Actually, I had first gone into Björk and Börjeson's antiquarian bookshop looking for something more on the subject of the French Revolution. An older gentleman approached me and asked me what I was looking for. But I didn't want to let on that I didn't know where they kept their history books, so I just pointed at the discount table in the middle of the room and said:

"I just want to look around a little."

"Go right ahead," he said and left.

There was nothing there about the French Revolution. They were mainly detective stories about Bulldog Drummond and the like. But there were also a few serious books, too. It was then that I bought the Emil Norlander book. I packed it along with the

other books in the chest I was taking to America. Just then the
door in the wall behind me bangs open. There is a draft in the
room, and I awaken, and sit up in bed. I have just dreamed something I didn't want to dream. The room is utterly silent and dark.
The door along the closet wall towards the corridor is properly
closed. The curtains are drawn, and as for the door in the wall
behind me, it was part of my dream and exists only as a feeling of
unpleasantness in the real room. The door was very high, and
when it opened, it was cold. But I don't know what I actually
dreamed.

It could be like that time last summer, when I woke up and
remembered that I had ten crowns hidden in the middle drawer of
the bureau in the room at Kvicksta. I knew it. I had a clear memory of how I held the banknote in my hand, pulled out the drawer
and placed the money under the shelf-paper in the left, inner corner. I then smoothed the paper out again, so that no one would
find it. But, later when I pulled out the drawer and lifted the shirts
that lay there, I saw that the paper was old and that it was secure-
ly fastened in the left inner corner with two rusty thumbtacks, and
I realized that what I remembered never was.

"I must have dreamed it."

Still, it was long into the afternoon that day before the memory faded to the normal proportions of a remembered dream. That
whole morning the memory of the crown note felt like the recollection of something real. It was perfectly solid and distinct. In a
way, I circled and poked at it as I thought about it, the way you
do with a tooth that is about to fall out. The memory was there,
like the tooth before it really loosened and could be spit out, with
the blood and all. You feel the tooth is there, and it can be
pushed back and forth, and bent, until it can be pried loose with
one of those really strong, sweet, deep and smarting pains.

There have been other such memories, recollections that have
been dreams, although they seemed real. I know this for a fact. I

can see them surface. But they were more threatening than a non-existent ten crown note in a dresser drawer. If they had been reality, my life would have been different, so I let them be. I don't poke around at them. This time, it wasn't like that at all, however. No, it was just the opposite. I don't know anything at all about what I had dreamed; it had left no trace in my memory. All that is left is a chill along my spine. As if there were still a draft blowing from far off through the wall behind me, as I sit up here, where there exists no high, open door and where I am not in any assembly and there is no mountain.

It's not true that I am afraid of the dark. I am not afraid of the dark. That was many years ago now. Perhaps I was when I was little. Still, there is a darkness which turns into an unpleasantness between my shoulder blades and in my neck. It's nothing I can talk about. But if I were to get out of bed, go toward the door, open it, and walk through the corridor, I would carry that darkness with me like some large, cold knapsack. I would feel the parquet floor and rug beneath my feet, and feel myself walk on the strip of brass that holds the carpet down, and there would never be any danger of me stumbling or walking into a wall, because I could see in the dark. I always sensed the wall in time. In the dark, one doesn't see, one perceives. The small, low obstacles and sharp, pointed objects that can be dangerous in the dark. I am unable to sense things like that. When it comes to objects like that, I have to rely on my memory and know where the chairs and small tables are located.

I have always known how to move about in the dark. But I have also practiced. You have to begin with eyes open in the pitch dark. It can't be done blindfolded, since that blocks perception and may cause one to stumble right into the wall with a crash. You have to practice at night, when it is dark, or in a closed room, where no light enters. It's no big deal to be able to move safely through the darkness. I believe it has something to do with

the density of the air. It feels as though the air grows more dense
just before I'm about to walk into a wall. It is the same, by the
way, when you close your eyes and slowly move the palm of your
hand toward a wall or tabletop. Just before the palm touches the
surface, you feel it. It kind of tickles. Then it is a matter of stop-
ping. Through practice, you can become adept at feeling and you
can walk around in the dark as surely as a bat flies. We have stud-
ied bats in school. They come out in the evening, at dusk. About
that time one can see them down in the yard around the fruit
trees at Kvicksta. During the day they hang upside-down beneath
the rafters in the barn and the old shed. They have a very peculiar
smell. When you enter a room with bats, you can smell them
immediately. Then you hear them. They scream to each other
when someone comes. I learned in school that one could blind
and mutilate them in various ways, and still they could make their
way unharmed across a dark room in which piano wire was
strung from wall to wall. They were able to hear and sense the
wires. Their senses are acute; mine are less finely tuned. I can
only sense walls and larger objects.

I have read about them as the Second Family: Smooth Noses
(gynorhina) in Brehm's *The Life of Animals*. Included were instructions on how to tame them. They can become quite devoted to
their master. I would like to have some tame bats, but I can't tell
anyone about it. People don't like them. They're afraid of bats.
Perhaps it's because of what's written in the Bible. In Leviticus,
Moses lists them among the unclean animals that are not to be
eaten.

I sit in bed and imagine them flitting by up there. I could call
them or whistle to them. And they would come flying to me on
their big bat-wings and perch on my shoulders. One on each side.
With their thumbs they would cling to my sweater and hang there.
I would speak to them reassuringly and they would squeak back
like field mice, and then I could send them away. People would

scream if they came upon them in the dark. It would be worse than letting mice loose on people. You can keep the mice hidden up your sleeve during the day, even at school. You just have to make sure that they don't stick their heads up out of your collar. You have to keep them down in your sleeve. They crawl around in there. Then, when you're ready, you shake them down into your hand and put them on people. The eyes of the mice sparkle and the victim screams in terror, especially the girls. If you put the mice down inside their blouse, they almost faint. A bat would be even better.

I sit there breathing in the dark room, my legs crossed on the bed. But I don't get up. I know that if I get up right now, I will have that cold knapsack of discomfort on my back. A cold hump to carry. I wouldn't call it fear. I'm not afraid of the dark. It's something else. It is like a feeling of chilly anticipation at my neck. It passes.

This business about being able to walk around in the dark is also something I can't speak about. It's a matter of not groping with your hands. The hands should be held perfectly still. They should rest. Instead, you should walk quietly throughout the unfamiliar darkness, sensing what is in front and to the side as if you had long antennae sticking out from the eyelids, ears, cheeks, neck, hands and (if you are barefoot, which is best) from the feet. You might think of them as invisible whiskers. I tried to explain this to Mary once, but I was unsuccessful.

Slowly, the darkness changes. The room begins to take shape again. It becomes possible to discern the curtains, floor, ceiling and walls. It is not until light begins to slip in around the edges of the curtains that I lie back and extend my legs. I must have fallen asleep the minute my head hit the pillow. And this time I did not dream. I just slept late, on this my first morning in America.

CHAPTER 10

On this first day in America, I am lying on my stomach up on a grassy slope in Van Cortland Park browsing through an issue of Mechanix Illustrated. I recall this clearly. The lawn has just been mowed. I looked for some four-leaf clover, but in vain. There is the smell of grass and American printing ink. American papers smell nothing at all like the ones in Sweden. They smell sweeter. I arrived in New York yesterday. But the leaves of the trees haven't turned yellow here yet, and it is late summer, not early autumn. Nevertheless, it is windy. And the air is so clear that I imagine I can see the leaves on the trees there to my left, though I know that I can't. The sky is a light blue, and I can inhale the air and fill my lungs. And the whole time, I smell the grass and the printing ink from the thick magazine I am reading. It was yesterday I arrived, and yet there is something about the time that doesn't jive.

I had helped with the dishes after lunch. I had dried. I couldn't just stand there talking and not lend a hand. The housekeeper was a blonde and laughed a lot. She was 25 and her name was Karna. She had gone in for sports and had been a swimmer. She wore glasses. They suited her. I liked her, even though she was a blonde. I liked the way she laughed. You could talk with her. She always knew what I meant. And she had a quick tongue. The only reason she had taken this position, working for Gunnar and and Alva, was so that she could come along and see America. She was actually a certified home economics teacher.

I had been talking about why work is destructive, while drying the dishes.

"The hard-working individual always meets with misfortune," I said.

It was idleness, in my opinion, that assured one a long, meaningful life. People had to break themselves of the habit of work.

"You're certainly doing your best," Karna said.

"I've read an article that proves it," I said. "I can show you if you don't believe me. It's full of graphs and charts. It includes statistics covering more than fifty years of life insurance data on American university students. Those who lived longest were the feeble, the sick, and the theology students. They did nothing all their lives, and lived peacefully, happily and healthily into their eighties. Those who were the first to die were the strong and healthy, and those who went in for sports. They worked and worked hard, and died like flies, after short, toilsome lives. Work and sports are extremely dangerous."

She laughed at me while I talked. She worked so fast that I could hardly keep up with her.

"You do have your theories," she said.

"They're scientifically proven," I insisted.

When Karna finished washing up, wiping off the sink and stove, swabbing the floor and putting everything away, she was free for the remainder of the afternoon.

"I'm going out to take a look at the city," she said. "Do you want to come with me?"

We turned to the left when we got out onto the street. It was a warm day and despite the traffic, there was a Sunday calm in the air. We took another left and walked up 116th street. The university was here. At the Columbia University subway station we took the uptown train to the end of the line. We found seats right away, since it was Sunday. The train swayed. At 122nd Street the train came out into the light. We could see the sidewalks far below us. To get to the station at 125th Street, people did not go downstairs, they had to climb sixty feet up from the street. At 135th Street the earth once more rose up around us and the train returned underground.

We must have come up again at 193rd Street, but I can't remember what it looked like there. Nor do I recall what we talked about, although I do know that we talked. Karna wore a tan beret, light summer coat, a plaid skirt and a white blouse. All that I remember is that I bought *Mechanix Illustrated* at the newsstand when we got off the train at the end of the line at 242nd Street. By then we had left the island Manhattan behind us and were in the Bronx.

We walk up to the park and Karna sits in the sun. She is bareheaded and when I look up from my *Mechanix Illustrated*, I notice that the breeze is blowing through her blond hair. Later, I seldom bought that magazine. It was the least expensive of its kind, and the thinnest. Here in America there were three different monthly magazines, thick like books, with pictures, text and lots of ads, all about technical questions and science. They also included instructions on how to build or alter your radio, how to build a model airplane or how to fix your car. I usually bought *Popular Science*. It had the best coverage of new inventions and discoveries. But I also often bought *Popular Mechanics*. These magazines were about 300 pages long.

I know for a fact that it is *Mechanix Illustrated* I am reading on this particular day. The magazine has just come off the press and it smells good. The pages almost stick to each other when I turn them, they are so fresh. Despite the breeze, I can feel the sun on my neck. But I can't really picture the cover or the article I am reading. However, if I look up from the magazine, to my right I see a large red brick building across the grass on the ridge. I believe it has a tower with pinnacle. It looks like an English manor, the kind you see in the small, brownish, oval pictures of the *Illustrated London News*. A hedge runs around the large house, and here, just by my side to the left, Karna sits with her face tilted up toward the sun. She leans back, her palms down on the grass, and closes her eyes. She has taken off her sunglasses, her eyelids are bare and her face perfectly naked. She is bare-headed; she has taken off her beret and placed it on her coat beside her. When she took off her coat, she said:

"If I don't take it off, I'll get grass stains on it; and that looks terrible."

Then she laughed. Now she has tilted her head, eyes closed, up towards the sun. Her blond hair blows in the breeze. I find her pretty and now that she's got her eyes closed, I can stare at her. It's as though a crumb of laughter remains at the corner of her mouth; she sits perfectly still. She has a fine mouth, with big lips. The downy hairs at the back of her neck are almost pure white. They gleam in the sunlight.

She holds her neck outstretched as as she leans her head back, and there are mother of pearl buttons on her blouse. She wears a thin silver chain around her neck. There at the opening, where the silver chain falls in under the blouse—between her breasts—she is tanned a tawny gold. Out of the corner of my eye, I also notice that her blouse is stretched taut across her breasts. I like her. But I am able to look back down at my *Mechanix Illustrated* in time, before she opens her eyes and looks at me.

"Did you know that we have cockroaches in the kitchen?" she says.

Before I can really grasp the meaning of her words, I note that she talks with a Gothenburg accent. She also hums the 's' sound slightly, I remark, while I listen to what she says about the cock-roaches, no longer concentrating on the sound of her voice.

"I thought I smelled something funny as soon as we got there yesterday, but when I woke up last night and went into the kitchen for a glass of water, I saw them when I turned on the light. And these were no ordinary cockroaches, either. They were big, shiny, reddish-yellow, disgusting creatures. They were several centimeters long. I could see how they moved their antennae around. And they were fast, too. I took a swipe at them, but they disappeared like greased lightning with a horrible rustle. They only come out at night, when it's dark."

After a moment she went on.

"Cockroaches are also difficult to get rid of. Once they've got into a house, it is usually almost impossible to get rid of them. A few years ago there was a bakery down in the Majorna in Gothenburg that was shut down by the health department because they had so many roaches. One evening when they made an unannounced inspection of the premises, the entire floor was covered with them. It was just one big rustling, crawling mass of cockroaches. Impossible to get rid of them. No matter what they tried, no matter how clean they kept the place, they were still there. They are stubborn animals; they have nine lives like cats. In the end, they had to tear the place down."

When we take the downtown train back home, we ride past our station and get off at 103rd Street.

"Let's wait two stations to get off," Karna had suggested. "We have time."

Leaving the station, we go down to Riverside Drive and walk the thirteen blocks up past 116th Street, to number 449. I have no memory of signs of autumn in the park. The buses drive by, double-deckers. The upper level on them is open. While a bus waits for a green light at 115th Street, I look at the people sitting up there. There is an elderly man in a black overcoat and black hat. A lady in a fur coat with two young girls. A man in his thirties without an overcoat, but wearing a gray hat, has his arm around a black-haired girl in a white blouse and red scarf. The weather must still have been warm, since they are dressed for summer. He points at something. I think I hear her laugh. Then the light changes and the bus drives on.

Walking here now, I notice what I didn't see yesterday; this was once a very fashionable neighborhood, but is now gradually losing its true elegance; it is fading (I use the Swedish word *changeras,* although I am not quite sure how it is pronounced), and becoming only semi-fashionable. Dented garbage cans stand at the street corners. They stink as you walk by, since their lids aren't properly closed and the garbage reeks.

I notice that some of the doormen, standing this late-summer afternoon in the doorways looking out on the street, park, river and passers-by, have stains on their uniforms. They are all Negroes. There is not one white doorman to be seen the entire way home. I also note that some of the façades of the buildings need repair. And there are cockroaches in these houses, large, rustling, shiny, red insects, that smell bad and leave an offensive odor on everything they touch. This is a street for sightseers—they come for the river—but I realize that this is no longer a really fashionable address.

As we walk up Riverside Drive, the twilight begins to dim. A cold wind off the river suddenly brings a chill, and darkness falls abruptly just as we arrive. When we get home, Karna goes to her room to change into her blue and white working smock and begin dinner. She has prepared it that morning. There is no dinner party this evening, just a simple Sunday dinner with Gunnar's assistant and his wife, as Alva put it. I set the table for them. I'm not doing it for the money, but to be able to talk a little more with Karna. When I'm done, I sit down on the kitchen sink, but she shoos me off.

"I don't have time to listen to you now," she says. "I don't know where everything is in the kitchen yet. I'm afraid I'll make a mistake if you go on talking."

I go into my room and browse through *Mechanix Illustrated* a little while. There's an article about a gyroplane. I like the picture. There is a woman flying a gyroplane inside a large sports arena. Then I return to the kitchen. But Karna is rushed.

"I don't have time for you right now."

The governess, my little sisters and I eat diced meat, onions and potatoes, and drink milk. The adults will eat later and will be served something else. But Karna has promised to save me some dessert. The adults are going to be having that flaming ice cream. Alva orders it sometimes for her dinner parties. I like it. It looks so fine as it burns with the dancing blue flames.

Karna had made the sponge-cake before lunch. It was in the refrigerator. Ice cream would be placed on it and the meringue, and then the whole thing was stuck in the oven. As she took it out of the oven, Karna would pour cognac over it and light it just before serving. It looked wonderful. There was hot chocolate sauce to pour over the dessert. But the flames die out quickly, the meringue gets soft, and the ice cream melts, so it has to be eaten right away. It should still be pretty good when I get my share.

As it grows darker and night falls, I stand at my window watching the lights going on in the apartments across the way. At eight o'clock, when the adults sit down to eat, it is already night.

CHAPTER 11

I look up from my book, out the train window across the aisle. The train is heading northwest in a curve, and I can see down into the valley. There are fenced-in fields for grazing. The large, black and white cows raise their heads and gaze up at the train. A road runs down there, following us. It draws near and drifts away again, then comes toward us once more. The white roadway between the green fields looks desolately empty. Only after a while do I see a car. We are traveling faster. We catch up and begin to pass. It is black. I think it is an old Ford. A lone man, dressed in overalls, is in the car, I think. The farmhouse in the distance is white with a red roof. And the barn (I use the English word) is painted white with a red roof. Now a brook. Or a drainage ditch. Beyond it, a bunch of houses. And factories. Actually, they look like small sheds. They look abandoned. There is a crisis. Or else they are just closed for the weekend. I catch a glimpse of a river ahead. We will soon be in Albany. But I don't have to change trains there. This car is going on to Buffalo. We go into a curve and I direct my attention to the interior of the coach instead.

The American railroad cars are different. They are not made up of small compartments, but are open, a bit like our streetcars, only much more modern. There is room for two passengers sitting abreast on either side of the aisle. We aren't seated on benches with room for two, but each on his own seat. However, I am the only one in my row now and have an unobstructed view through both windows. I sit in the outer seat on the left of the aisle. My ticket is stuck into the top of the headrest of the seat in front of me. The man seated there is bald. He is asleep, snoring. I see the ticket outlined against the man's lumpy head. There are twenty rows of seats in the car, I have counted them—one row per window. There is room for eighty passengers, but there are now only twenty-three of us: 20 men and three women. This, too, I have counted.

It is Friday afternoon, September 16, 1938, and I am on my way north through the state of New York, to visit the university student who invited me that time I dropped in on Gunnar on board the MS *Kungsholm*. Not that I'm sure I really was invited; maybe it was just something they said in America. But Gunnar has phoned Syracuse to tell them I am coming, and they have promised to meet me. The bald man has left the train. He was just going to Albany.

I can picture the car and the heads in front of me, and I know that I am sitting in the eighth row. I should have definitely taken some other book with me to Syracuse. This one can't hold my attention. I hold the book, green cover up, on my knees, and look at the railroad car. I have my suitcase next to me. It's made of brown leather and is collapsible. It once belonged to my paternal grandfather and Grandmother gave it to me last year because I liked it. It's also practical, since it is lightweight. In it I have my toothbrush and soap, a change of socks, underwear, and an extra shirt. As I sit there in 1938 I know the name of the student, the name of the city he lives in and of the station where I am to get off. It's beyond Albany, not far from Syracuse. But now, looking back on it 45 years later, I cannot recall those names, not of the city, not of the family, not of the student.

I am riding north on the New York Central Line, in a day coach made entirely of steel. It has no open platforms with gates, like the Swedish railroad cars. The Swedish cars are extremely dangerous in the event of an accident. It's like taking a sledge-hammer to a matchbox. The passengers don't stand a chance. Here in America, the trains are safe. What is more, these cars are bogie wagons. I got a quick look at the bogies before I was put on the train. They were equipped with sturdy coil springs. I also bent down to examine the connection between the cars, since they used a different sort of coupling and no buffers, as we did. But they pulled at me and got me up again and wondered what I was doing. I just answered:

"Nothing."

"Then hurry up!" they said.

"Make sure you get off at the right station," they told me later.

And they pushed me up into the train. I waved, and went and sat down. But I had managed to get a look at the railroad cars from the outside as I walked along the platform. They were a very dark green with black roofs. Above the row of windows, NEW YORK CENTRAL LINE was written in gold. The car was number 409. The number hung below the washroom window. Those numerals, too, were painted gold. I believe the bogie drove a generator.

I should be reading a book written in English, but I am still unable to read the language easily. So I have chosen a Swedish book to take along on the trip. But I did choose a book in Swedish written by an American. The author is Jack London. He wrote a number of good books that I enjoyed reading. He wrote *The Iron Heel*, and books about Alaska and the South Seas. Now I was reading his short stories. I had brought this book with me from Sweden. But I wasn't enjoying it. That's why I later left the book in the room where I stayed at the student's house outside Syracuse. I never mentioned it, I just pretended that I had forgotten it.

I actually disliked the book. I didn't know Jack London wrote that kind of thing. What I was now reading was rather unpleasant. It was about this couple so much in love that they didn't even touch each other. They just lay there with a little space between them, their hands above the covers, saying how much they loved each other, never once touching. I felt ashamed as I read this, and I leafed through the book for a new story. But I only remember this one, the one that made me feel ashamed.

When I look out the window, the countryside has changed. Here the hills are covered in forest. I hear the rail joints. They haven't begun to weld the rails together here yet. They do that on the lines where the streamlined high-speed trains are going to run. They go 100 miles an hour. In Sweden, we would say 160 kilometers an hour. Some travel even faster. The book I'm reading is not good. The stories seem to get worse, the more I read. The conductor walks by again. I point to the ticket stuck high up on the headrest of the seat in front of me and go on reading. But he wants to see it again. I look up. It is not the same conductor. This one is fat. The one from New York City was thin. I start to say that the ticket is there, and I point. But as I say it, I see that there is no longer a ticket up on the headrest. It must have fallen to the floor. I bend down and look. The conductor says something. Again he asks to see my ticket. I try to explain everything to him. I can hear that my English is poor. My tongue won't do what I want it to do. He looks at me. I can hear my bad pronunciation, and try to keep my lower jaw in the right position, try to talk more back and up in my mouth. I notice that I am placing the words in the wrong order. I grope for words, and don't find them. His eyes are expressionless.

I explain where I am coming from and where I am going; I tell him what my ticket looked like and what the thin conductor had done the times he had come by, asked to see my ticket, examined it, clipped it and then stuck it up on the headrest of the seat in front of me. I realize that they are going to put me off at the next station. It can't be helped. Those are the rules.

A woman now approaches. She has been sitting three rows behind me. She says that it's true that the boy had a ticket. She gesticulates. She is short and has black hair and looks Italian. You can't just throw him off the train, she says. That wouldn't be right. He is a poor European boy, who has had some bad luck.

"I saw the ticket!"

Several people now gather around me and the conductor. My English is bad. I think it's getting worse. A feeling of shame sits like a soft, thick, disgusting lump in my throat, hindering my speech. An elderly man with a large white face, leans over me and asks me what happened. He speaks very gently, and I can see by his collar that he is a clergyman. I try to find the right words, but don't call him Father, since he is not a Catholic. I don't want to sound angry or indignant, and I especially wish to avoid appearing unsure of myself or anxious. I'm afraid people will start to pity me. Rather than have them feel sorry for me, I would smile amicably, be polite and get off at the next station, and then see what happened. In a hundred years we're all going to be dead anyway, so what's so important about one small ticket? Suddenly I see us all dead and gone. The entire train is actually in some museum someplace, like in the story H.G. Wells wrote about how he traveled into the future, where he saw his own tools and machines displayed as strange prehistoric objects. But he saw them in a museum that itself had become an abandoned prehistoric relic. Above all, just act natural. Show no emotion. Just sit here, smiling amicably, and try to master the words and pronunciation. After all, the worst that could happen is that I could die. If you were standing off to the side behind the display case window, looking in, and if this were all taking place long ago, it would be of no significance. A scrap of paper lost in this strange museum train, some time in the past.

Things like this happen. It can happen to anyone. It's not because I am a European immigrant, not because I am a boy. I don't want anyone pitying me, and if I just spoke the words better, no one would laugh at me. But no one is laughing. The clergyman with the big, pallid face explains that the thin conductor, on his last round before leaving the train, had taken my ticket by mistake. Or someone else had taken it. There are evil people who think doing things like taking the ticket of a poor European boy without his noticing it when they get off the train is some kind of practical joke, says the short, black-haired lady, who I think is Italian.

In any case, the ticket is not on the floor. Nor is it in any of my pockets or on my seat. It is just gone. They talk back and forth. There are now about a dozen adult Americans gathered around the conductor and me. They all defend me. The train pulls into a curve, the car sways. The clergyman grabs on to the headrest in front of me and says.

"One cannot just throw a boy off the train like that!"

A middle-aged man in a gray flannel suit points out that the boy is to be met at the station, and the simplest thing would be to let him continue on to his destination and see to it that someone picks him up. Finally, the conductor agrees to try to arrange it and writes out a new ticket. He hands it to me and says:

"But don't you lose this one, too!"

It is almost dark when I arrive. Someone must have met me, but I don't remember. Nor do I remember what the room I slept in looked like. But the house itself was painted white, with a large porch in front, in a suburb of houses with big lawns. There were fences between them, but no fences facing the street. But I do remember dinner; it was the first time I had eaten in an American home.

The dining room was very light, with yellow wallpaper and white curtains at the windows. A pair of sconces, for three lights each, hung on the inner long wall. The sconces were made of brass. They were scrolled, and small brass maple leaves hung from them. The light, of course, was electric. Along the other long wall, a white sideboard stood between two windows. Two real candles in silver candlesticks stood on it. From the ceiling a chandelier hung directly above the white oval dining room table with its six chairs. The chairs had high backs and seats of blue cloth.

The table seated ten, but the other four chairs were lined up along the inner wall between the sconces.

There were six of us at the table. At one end, with his back to the kitchen door, sat the student's father. He was about 60. He was stout, with a high complexion, and short, gray hair. He wore horn-rimmed glasses. I believe he was a real-estate agent, a *realtor*. At the other end of the table sat the student's mother. Actually she didn't really sit much. Instead, she ran back and forth between kitchen and dining room, bringing in and taking out the large serving dishes. She was thin and her hair gray. She had large eyes. I sat on one side of the table, with the student to my left and his mother to my right. Behind me there was a window looking out on the yard. Opposite me sat the student's younger brother. He was about my age. His sister sat between him and his father. She was thirteen or fourteen. She wasn't dressed like a young girl anymore; she wore a tight, high-necked blue sweater. You could see that she had begun to develop breasts. I tried not to let anyone see me looking. I think she had also begun to use lipstick. She helped her mother remove the dishes. She also carried in things like sauce and preserves. The table setting was different from what I was used to. Each of us had three plates: a large one, a smaller one to the left, and a still smaller one above it. On the smallest plate there lay a knife. There were two forks to the left of the big plate, a large fork on the outside and a small one near the plate. To the right of the plate lay a knife and spoon. There was a small spoon above the plate, and up to the right was a glass, which the student's mother filled with ice water from a large clinking glass pitcher. Everyone drank ice water and nothing else.

After a while, I realized that the smallest plate was meant for bread and butter. You took a slice of bread and placed it on the bread plate and then put a ball of butter beside it. Then you broke the bread into small pieces as you ate, placing a dab of butter with your own butter knife on the piece you were about to eat.

Clearly, it was not good form to spread a whole slice of bread and take bites out of it. You could only spread and eat one small morsel at a time. The medium-sized plate was for salad. They ate their salad here just the way Gunnar and Alva did. The small fork that lay furthest in was used for the salad. But I didn't like salad back then either, and when some was put on my plate and a pink dressing was poured over it, I poked a little at it with my fork, pretending to eat some, and said that it was:

"So very good!"

The student's mother carried in a tray with six small bowls of soup. This soup looked like gruel. It was made of corn and small bits of fried ham. It was quite good. It also had a slight taste of onion. When we had finished, the student's sister took our bowls and the mother came in carrying the main course on a silver tray with handles.

It was a meatloaf, with heaps of mashed potatoes piled around it. Around the rim of the platter large, boiled tomatoes had been arranged to form a wreath. The student's brother licked his lips and said:

"Real meatloaf!"

When the mother placed the platter next to the father, he smiled, took the ketchup bottle and began to shake ketchup over the meatloaf and potatoes, until everything was drenched in the red sauce. Then the mother cut him a piece and put it on his plate. He took a big gulp of ice water and began to eat, without waiting for the rest of us.

I was totally fascinated watching him eat. He ate almost the same way I did. But more carefully. First he picked up the fork in his left hand and the knife in his right. He stuck the fork into the big slice of meatloaf and, with the knife, cut off a small piece, bite-sized. He freed his fork and laid the knife at the upper edge of his plate. He then put his fork down in the middle of the plate. He put his left hand under the table, picked up the fork with his right hand, held it as if it were a spoon, and carried the piece of meatloaf to his mouth. He took some mashed potatoes with his fork, still holding it like a spoon in his right hand, while he chewed the meat. He carefully squeezed the mashed potatoes between the fork's four tines, lubricated the lump with ketchup and brought it to his mouth. With rapid movements of his lips, he cleaned off his fork. Then he put the newly cleaned fork on the plate and brought up the hand he had held hidden under the table. He now took the fork with his left hand, turned it and held down the slice of meatloaf, while he used his right hand to cut it with the knife. Then, once again, he put the knife down at the upper edge of the plate, pulled the fork out of the meat, put it on the plate in front of him and replaced his left hand to cut it with the knife. Then, once again, he put the knife down at the upper edge of the plate, pulled the fork out of the meat, put it on the plate in front of him and put his hand back under the table. At the same time, he took the fork with his right hand. This time he didn't turn it like a spoon, but instead jabbed it down toward the plate, speared the piece of meatloaf and carried it to his mouth, turning the fork so that the meatloaf was held by the tines. I noted that the fork had to lie untouched and had to be free of food before changing hands. He didn't allow the fork to hold either meatloaf or mashed potatoes, except when he was gathering food with it or lifting the food to his mouth. From time to time, he lifted the napkin from his lap, wiped the ketchup from his lips and took big gulps of ice water, without leaving traces of his lips on the glass. Several times he broke off a small piece of the bread which was on the smallest plate, buttered it, picked it up with the finger-tips of his right hand, and stuffed it quickly into his mouth. He swallowed it in one bite, without letting his fingers touch his lips.

The student's brother, sitting opposite me, didn't bother cutting his meatloaf with his knife. He didn't even touch his knife. It lay there next to his plate, like some ornament, all through the

meal. He used only his fork. He cut the meatloaf with his fork the
way you cut a piece of cake when you eat in a coffee shop. But
he kept his left hand hidden beneath the table the whole time. As
for the sister and mother, they ate like the father, and when I
sneaked a look at the student sitting next to me, I saw that he ate
pretty much like his father, although he forgot himself at times and
did like his little brother.

All I really had to do in order to eat like a genuine American
was keep my left hand under the table and not have food on the
fork when I changed hands.

After we finished the main course, the mother and sister
removed the dishes. I don't remember what the mother was wearing, but the sister had a dark blue pleated skirt. A white leather
belt separated the tight light blue sweater from the full, dark blue
skirt. She also wore silk stockings. I noticed that she had some
trouble getting the seams straight. The stockings sagged a little
around the knees. I took a quick look at her when she carried out
the dishes (perhaps she wasn't wearing a garter belt beneath her
skirt), but hastily looked away out through the window when she
came in with the dessert bowls. I didn't want her to notice or to
think that I was staring.

Now we were served ice cream. It was homemade. The student said that it was his mother's special ice cream, the kind she
made for birthdays. Now she had fixed it for me. It was made
with maple syrup and chopped walnuts. We each were served a
small bowl of this ice cream.

"This is the only place you can find genuine maple syrup,"
said the father. "It's a tradition from colonial times. When the pil-
grim fathers came here they discovered that the Indians used the
sap of the maple to sweeten their food. Since then we have
tapped the sugar maple and boiled the sap into syrup or maple
sugar. You can only do that with the real American maple."

Everyone at the table now asked me whether I liked maple

syrup ice cream.

"It's my mother's very own recipe," said the sister. "She learned it from her grandmother, who came from a very old family from Bangor, up in Maine. Maple syrup, whipping cream and eggs. Plus chopped nuts, a pinch of salt and some vanilla. The trick is to blend in the egg whites and whipping cream when the other ingredients are chilled and are beginning to freeze. I've also learned how to make it."

"We make it in the refrigerator now," said the mother. "But when I was a girl, I got to turn the ice cream in an ice cream freezer, with ice and salt. But most of the time we just made regular ice cream. This kind is special."

"It is a very good ice cream," I said.

And I heard my own words. I felt ashamed at how stilted I sounded, ashamed of my breathless intonation. Everyone could hear that I was a foreigner. A *Scandihoovian*. But they were all smiles around the table, and the brother said:

"It is also very *expensive*. You have to use real maple syrup. It takes over forty gallons of sap to make one gallon of syrup, and each tree gives only twelve gallons of sap per year. So on order to get one gallon of maple syrup, you have to tap three trees for a whole year."

"That's why the maple syrup they sell in New York City is diluted," said the father. "But up here we use only the real thing."

"People here are as proud of the sugar maple as you Swedes are of the oak trees in Stockholm," said the student. "The sugar maple is the official tree of the city of New York."

"I'm glad you liked the ice cream," said the mother. "We made it so that you could try something really American."

She got up from the table and went into the kitchen. She returned with a second portion for me. She had had it ready. The younger brother looked longingly at this new little bowl of genuine maple syrup ice cream that was now brought in to me. But he didn't ask for a second portion.

"Dig in and enjoy it," said the father. "In Europe you have nothing like it."

I have but one more recollection from this visit. I am sitting in the front seat of the family car. It was a Pontiac station wagon. The chassis, with the hood, windshield and fenders, was like that of most cars, but on it there was a body with a frame of white maple and sides of black mahogany. The roof was of steel for safety's sake. It was only in America that I saw such cars. They seated more passengers than a regular car, and could carry as much luggage as a small truck. In this station wagon there was room for seven adults, not counting the driver. Of course, if they were children and not adults, still more could fit.

"When we drove to the Fourth of July celebration, there were twelve of us!" says the brother.

The student drives. His brother sits in the back. His sister is not here. The younger brother talks about James Fenimore Cooper and the Pathfinder. We drive along a black asphalt road, up a hill and through a grove of tall maples. Their trunks are white. Their leaves burn yellow, red and bronze. It's a sunny day and the air is almost unbelievably clear. I roll down the window and the breeze blowing on me is cool, not cold. Still, it is here in this grove of maples in upstate New York that I first experienced an American fall. I see the leaves on the ground. The layer of leaves lies like an orange carpet along the black asphalt. I see the white trunks and how the bronze-colored leaves, two by two, flutter down through the clear air under pale blue sky. And I feel the freshness in my nostrils and the smell of moss.

When we arrived in America the week before, the leaves couldn't have already changed color down by the Hudson in New York City. Not down there, not on the first of September. That memory must be wrong. It's here and now as I roll down the window and the student shifts to a lower gear up the hill as the road curves over the ridge and the forest stretches out before us—it is at this moment that I experience an American autumn for the first time. The maples are very tall. I turn to the younger brother and say that Leif, Erik the Red's son, took maple logs from trees such as these home with him to Brattahlid, when the storms drove him to Finland and he discovered America, 838 years ago.

"It is written that some of the logs were so big they could be used to build houses," I said. "There wasn't much timber to be had on Greenland. They must have been maples like these."

But I was having difficulty with my English. Some of the words I needed just weren't there. First I had to think of them in Swedish and then search for them in English. I don't think the brother understood what I was saying. He just nodded and said:

"Of course."

I could picture them making their way through the forest. Leif had large, bulging pop-eyes, a braided beard and a yellow moustache. He was shouting, his mouth wide open. He wore leg wrappings and in his right hand carried a short sword of the type popular then. The others came tramping behind. But they never actually got this far south or inland. And I didn't know the younger brother well enough to go on telling him more about them. Besides, my English wasn't good enough, either.

I feel a scratching in my palm. I look away from the maple grove we are driving through. We have been in the city. We have visited a big store with toys, games, models, fish and other animals. I have bought a turtle. It cost 25 cents. It has a rose on its shell. Not a real rose, but a decalcomania rose, the type girls use on their books or letter paper. You take the piece of paper with the rose on it, place it in water and then put it face down on the book page, letter paper or whatever, then you carefully remove the paper. I know the word in Swedish, although not many people use it. Here in America they simply say decal. Actually, I'm sorry the little turtle has the rose on his shell. You shouldn't do things like that to animals. It's not right to play or joke with nature. And a rose is certainly inappropriate. But I chose the turtle with the least offensive decoration, and when I get home I can wash off the decalcomania. It is a little undignified. The turtle rests in my palm. It has stuck out its head and looks around with a quick jerk. His legs are out too; they were what scratched me. When I cup my hand around this little turtle so as not to lose him, he immediately pulls in his head and legs again.

"It's easy to build," says the brother. "I have one just like it."

He is referring to the model airplane. He helped me choose the model I bought. It was actually a competition model. According to the text on the carton, its design was based on the experience of many competitions. It was primarily meant as a glider. It had a rubber-band motor, of course, to get it high enough in the air, but the propeller folded up as soon as the rubber band lost its tension, and then spun freely so as not to create air resistance, allowing the plane to fly a long distance. The model was extremely light: it weighed just a little over four ounces (about 130 grams), despite its 41 inch wingspan. it was quite expensive, actually. It cost $1.50. He had the package there in the backseat.

"We can compete at home tomorrow," he said. "If we build it tonight, we can take both planes to the field early tomorrow and fly them before we go to church. No one's playing there then."

But I didn't intend to build it until I got back to New York City. It was difficult to carry it on the train, once it was built. It was quite fragile. Suddenly, without warning, someone would stick a cane through the paper, and then everything was ruined. What is more, I didn't want him around when I built the plane. This particular model was quite demanding. It wasn't so difficult to steam and bend balsa wood, but I wanted to be alone when I stretched the paper. I would fly it in some park. Perhaps I could fly it in the park near the house on Riverside Drive.

We don't see many cars on this road. It is actually a parkway.

It's straight now and climbing. The student downshifts again. The engine is not in the best of shape. My Uncle Folke would have been able to fix it. I imagine that I have built the model plane. Now I am winding it up, my finger at the propeller. I hold the model in my hand. I let the propeller go and at the same time throw the plane. It soars toward the blue sky. I see it climb over the treetops. It flies high up there. It comes down, sweeps over the treetops, and then descends in a long, long glide down towards the woods. I see it make a fine, smooth landing up ahead on the black asphalt. The climb becomes so steep that the student has to shift to first gear. He double clutches and the engine revs an instant before continuing its hacking.

"We're going to buy a new car in the winter," the brother says.

The train pulls into Grand Central Station on Tuesday afternoon, and I am expecting someone will be there to meet me. My hosts have telegraphed to say I am arriving and which train I will be on. I prepared to get off long before we arrive. I put on my cap and stood up as soon as we went into the tunnel, and now stand, with my grandfather's leather suitcase in hand, right by the door. I am first. The other passengers form a line behind me. We pull in so the left-hand door leads out to the platform. As the train slows down, I look out the window in the door. Several porters are waiting there with their carts. They are wearing red caps. When the train stops, an elderly gentleman behind me opens the door. He reaches past me and won't allow me to open it. But I'm first out of the train anyway. I look up and down the platform. It is soon crowded with passengers. There is no one there I recognize. I start to walk towards the exit. By the time I've walked the length of two railroad cars, I realize no one is there to meet me.

It's essential that no one discovers this. I mustn't let it show. Therefore, I can't allow myself to slow down. Nor can I begin to run or look around. I must walk at the same pace as before, looking straight ahead. It should appear as though I am walking the way I always do, thinking about something else. Otherwise, the danger is that someone will approach and start talking to me. Ask me who I am and where I am going. In this gigantic station, they have a special service with staff out on the platforms looking for children and young women to help. In particular, they are out to save young women who have never been to New York City before and who don't know where to stay. But they also help lost children. They mustn't catch sight of me. I don't want them to notice me and pick me up. I walk down the platform with my little leather suitcase. It is light and it mustn't appear a burden.

The platform is very crowded now. It is swarming with people. They have suitcases and carry their coats folded over their arms. They have umbrellas and gray bags. The men who walk by are wearing gray suits, white shirts and ties, and they stare out into space with blank expressions. They are in a hurry. I put on the same blank expression. I don't allow my gaze to settle on anyone or anything; I just make my observations from the corner of my eye and keep walking. A short, middle-aged woman, in a yellow dress and a large black hat drags a brown suitcase with one hand and a screaming child with the other. The child is about four years old. A boy. He strains and resists, and she pulls him along. He digs in his heels and screams. Many of the men carry their newspapers pressed against their sides, under their arms. There are so many of us walking straight ahead that it is almost jammed. They tramp along all around me. We all march in step toward the exit and station hall.

This is Grand Central Terminal. Suddenly I picture it above the gray hats grinding their way toward the exit. First I see it from the outside, like in a photograph, with the great clock and all the sculpture up around the roof, and then I see it from above, like on a map. Here we have Manhattan, and there is Grand Central Terminal, between 42nd and 45th Streets. Park Avenue splits around the enormous station. It was built in 1913. Six hundred trains arrive and depart from here daily. Here 3000 railroad cars let out their passengers every day. The depot is underground. It stretches 25 blocks uptown. There are two levels of platforms here. Trains come and go around the clock. There is a continual rumble above the sound of tramping feet. I think I can feel the trains beneath the soles of my shoes. Now we are almost out in the station hall, and I must decide what to do, without being noticed. The minute I hesitate, I become visible.

There are buses and subways from down here that go uptown to where we live at 116th Street and Riverside Drive. I have enough money left to take the Fifth Avenue bus if I want. It costs a dime, ten cents. The subway only costs a nickel.

There is a movie theater here, a barber and various shops, and a news vendor at a large stand, featuring all kinds of papers and magazines. The covers are colorful and, like everyone else, I turn my head toward the newspaper stand and take a look at the covers with the girls, cars, planes and more girls—the kind that are only in bathing suits or less. I look furtively at them, as I continue walking, suitcase in hand, without changing my stride.

The station is huge. The enormous hall is an entire space filled with the high-pitched, noisy buzz of hundreds of people, and through the windows above, the sun sends great beams of light across the dusty air. Not a moment of hesitation now, eyes devoid of expression. I let them go so blank that the skin on my cheeks feels tight and my lips prickly. I could take the bus. I have taken that line once before, although not from here. I had come in a taxicab, because they prefer to travel that way; but I can't afford it.

The buses are double-deckers. If you sit up on top, you have a view. You sit out in the open. It's nice, if the weather is good. Those who want to smoke and, of course, all the sightseers, sit on the wooden seats above. No standing is allowed on these buses. That's why they are twice as expensive as other means of transportation. We took the bus to Rockefeller Center the day we went sightseeing. I ran up the stairs to be first, but I still didn't succeed in getting a seat in one of the front rows. Four ladies were already sitting there. Two on one side of the aisle and two on the other. They had been out shopping and had various kinds of bags with them. Two of them were bare-headed, while one wore a little black hat. But the one who sat furthest to the right, just in front of me, had on a hat that looked like a big blue bird with spread wings. I wondered what you would say to her if she were sitting in front of you at the movies. The benches were yellow. Toward the aisle, there was a sturdy bluish-black iron grip at the top of the bench. If the bus swerved, you could grab onto it. But you weren't allowed to stand while the bus was moving.

On that occasion we had driven up Fifth Avenue, past Central Park, to 110th Street, where we crossed over to Riverside Drive. We then followed it all the way home. I could see our new home a long way off. I saw the high, black, iron fence in front of the buildings on the next block. The unemptied garbage cans. 116th Street climbing a hill to the right.

But I don't know where to catch the Fifth Avenue bus. I must ask, and I don't want to do this. They will hear that I am a foreigner, and they will say that I am

A lost child.

If that's the way they say it. Perhaps they would say

This boy has got lost.

But I am not *lost.* I know where I am and how I can leave this place and I certainly don't need any help. I could also take the subway. A shuttle runs from here to Times Square, where I can change to the line that runs uptown along the west side of Manhattan. But I'm not exactly sure how to do it. I mean, I do know how to get to the subway. But then I'll have to look at a map. And if I stood there looking at it, someone would come up and ask me where I was going.

I walk quickly and calmly, following the crowd. They lead me out onto 42nd Street, I see. I have given absolutely no indication that as I walk here with my suitcase, I am trying to figure out how to get home. I picture Manhattan in my mind. I am now coming out onto 42nd Street, down by Vanderbilt Avenue. Up ahead runs Park Avenue, around the station and north. Actually, I could also head north on Park Avenue, then west until I came to Central Park, up along the park, turning off on 116th Street and proceeding until I got to Riverside Drive. But here I am, already on 42nd Street; the light changes and I follow the crowd and have already crossed Vanderbilt Avenue. So I continue west on 42nd Street. I will cross Madison Avenue and Fifth Avenue, where I should be able to catch a bus (but won't). Then only Sixth Avenue remains before I come out on Broadway, which I follow diagonally, up towards Times Square.

I walk along 42nd Street. First I have to walk four blocks west and then 74 blocks north on Broadway. But since Broadway doesn't run perfectly straight, you could say that it is about 77 blocks to walk on Broadway. At 116th Street, I will turn west and then it is two more blocks to Riverside Drive. Although it might also be considered only one block, since there is no cross street on the southern side of 116th Street, between Broadway and Riverside Drive. Then I go north again, and it's half a block home. It's about as far as from Skansen to Olovslund in Stockhom, a distance I've walked. Walking at a normal pace, I should be home around dinnertime.

That afternoon I make my way up along Broadway with my suitcase. What I remember most clearly is my suitcase. It doesn't really go together with a stroll in the city. It announces that I am from the country. For this reason, I must walk along and not attract attention to myself. I blend in with the stream of pedestrians. We stop for a red light. The traffic rushes past. The light changes and we set off again.

From time to time, there is a shop window I would like to stop and look at. But I don't. I don't even stop near 97th Street, where the show window is full of puppies. But I notice that my pace slackens. People walk by me. I have turned my head and looked in the window. The puppies climb over each another. I hear them yapping through the glass They don't bark. They are too young. It's not right to take a litter that early. They shouldn't be there, on the sawdust in the shop window. Animals shouldn't be treated that way. They don't look like purebreds, but might be English beagles. They are white and brown, with drooping ears. They tumble over each other. One of them gets up and leans its front paws against the window pane. It looks me straight in the eye as I walk by. I feel those great big dog eyes in the very pit of my stomach, but I still don't stop. I just keep walking straight ahead, trying to keep the same pace. Nor do I stop in front of the movie theaters, even though I would like to look at the posters and photos. But far up Broadway, near 110th Street, I see the *NEMO* theater on the other side of the street. This is the theater closest to home. I have seen it advertised in the newspaper. Now I know where it is located. I'll go here later, I think to myself.

As I turn off Broadway onto 116th Street, I see the sun going down over a distant New Jersey. For a minute the sun hangs large and red above the tree top, and then swiftly sinks into the veils of smoke. At the same time, the trees in park begin to loom higher, concealing more and more of the evening sky, the further west I progress along the northern side of 116th Street.

I turn the corner and come out on Riverside Drive, continuing north. I arrive at 449 Riverside Drive just as the doorman is opening the door. Gunnar and Alva are on their way out. They are wearing evening dress. The taxi is already there waiting.

"But Jan!" says Alva. "Aren't you home? Where have you been?"

"I've walked from the station," I say.

"But *darling,* you promised to pick him up," she says to Gunnar.

At first I think he is going to tell her he forgot. It's as if he hesitates for just one second. But then he replies:

"I received this strange telegram saying that Jan is arriving with the Turtle and Airplanes at Grand Central at 3:20. You know trains have such strange names these days, so I asked someone to phone from the office and to find out whether the *Turtle and Airplane* was late. But the person at the station said that there was no such train, so I just took it for granted that the telegram was a joke."

He isn't talking, he's rattling it off rather monotonously. He sounds like a boy caught at some prank. As though he has been caught playing a practical joke and is now trying to excuse himself. The whole time he looks at me with his aqua blue eyes I know he is lying. But he doesn't call it lying, talking this way. He might say that he is fooling around, or that it is a joke, or that he is teasing. But I don't let on that I understand. I say nothing at all.

"But *darling,*" says Alva, with her flutelike girlish laugh, "you mustn't be so absentminded."

She says this with a dismissive gesture of her right hand. She is wearing shiny black gloves of fine leather. But her eyes are stony. Her pupils are contracted. She is afraid.

"Jan can take care of himself," says Gunnar.

I smile. That's what I always do these days, when things happen like this. I look past them, through them and just smile. Gunnar gets out his wallet and takes out two dollars. He holds them out in his hand a moment so I can see them. Then he puts one of the dollars back onto his wallet and gives me the other.

"Here, this is to make up for it," he says.

"*Darling,* you're impossible," says Alva, again, with her high-pitched laugh. Her pupils, however, are still stony.

"Run along upstairs, now," Gunnar tells me.

"Hurry up, darling," he says to Alva.

They turn toward the car and the cab driver leans across the front seat, sticks out his hand and opens the car door. I start in through the big glass door, which is still held open by the Negro doorman with the red uniform. I can see them in the glass. As they get into the cab, they are mirrored there, along with the marble floor and the elevator's brass grating, behind and through them. The car door swings shut and they drive away. I could see that they were going to an elegant dinner party. Alva was wearing one of those floor-length gowns, metallic silver beneath her black coat, and Gunnar had his doctor's hat.

On the way up in the elevator, I think to myself that this is something I could never tell anyone about. Gunnar thinks it amusing to do things like this. It's like the time when I was a little child and afraid of drowning. Gunnar took me on his shoulders and swam way out. It was in the archipelago. It was a cold summer's day in 1934. The sky was gray and a hard wind was blowing. The rocks were extremely slippery and I had lost my footing as he chased me. When I fell and he caught me, I screamed. Alva told him to be careful and he assured her that I was screaming because it was so much fun. And he caught me and put me on his shoulders, and headed straight out into the deep water with me. He began to swim and I twisted and howled. He held tight to me. The wind was so heavy that there were whitecaps on the water, and we were far, far out, so that I could barely see the shiny gray rocks beneath the ashen sky. He dove so that the water closed over my head, the whole time keeping hold of me, and when I came to the surface I was no longer screaming, I just hiccupped. Since then I have never cried in front of him. I wouldn't give him the pleasure. Suddenly, in the elevator mirror, I see the vast, cold sea, and how the waves splash toward me with white foam and hear Gunnar laughing as he pulls me under. Jokes like this are the only thing besides his scientific achievements that he finds amusing. No one can understand this. No one outside our family knows what our family is really like. I could not even tell my paternal grandmother. She wouldn't want to listen. She would just tell me I shouldn't pay any attention to it, and that Alva and Gunnar are like that, and that they don't mean anything by it. But I know that Gunnar really does mean something by it. And Grandmother knows it too, though she won't admit it. I know that she knows. I have heard her talking about Gunnar and Alva, talking to my other grandmother.

"Lova, try to understand how it feels," she said, crying.

The entire family knows about it. But you can't say anything or mention it to outsiders. I can't talk about it with anyone. Ever.

Still, it's not really such a big deal. You can resist. Grandmother doesn't understand that it's a matter of not allowing yourself to be weak. The other members of the family are weak. They're afraid of him. Even grandmother is afraid. But me he can't touch.

"This family is degenerating," Gunnar had said, while drinking coffee with all his brothers and sisters, and their spouses, after the traditional family dinner on the day after Christmas.

He had put down his coffee cup and pointed at me.

"Father could bend horseshoes with his bare hands, but Jan can't even play football."

Alva laughed.

"Oh, but *darling*," she said.

I didn't say anything. I stood by the bookshelf and leafed through the thick, red, French encyclopedia that lay by the telephone. I was looking at the pictures. On the cover a girl blew on a dandelion flower, spreading the seeds on the wind. When I heard what Gunnar had said, I turned so that everyone could see my face, so they could see that I hadn't even changed my expression. Gunnar ate a ginger snap and looked at me. I wondered if he meant to continue.

The others said nothing. Then Gunnar's younger brother tried to say that it was still hard to tell. He wanted to defend me.

"He's still only in the fourth grade."

"Sure, dear brother," Gunnar said, looking at him. "You mean well. But you have always thought with your heart. A child who isn't able to find his own playmates by the time he is ten, or a man who hasn't made some intellectual contribution of lasting value by the time he is 25, will never amount to anything. Don't you agree?"

Nobody answered. They all looked down into their coffee cups, except for Alva, who gave a little laugh.

Gunnar took another ginger snap and said:

"Why, his rectum wasn't even properly developed at birth. Doctor Renk from Strängnäs had to force it open with his thumb. You all remember that. His glands are to blame."

Gunnar held the ginger snap and looked at me as he said this. But I looked past him, out toward the apple tree, through the small round window by the fireplace. There they had mortared into the wall the cast Gunnar received from Trondheim. It was from the cathedral there. A devil carrying off a naked woman. It was a small medieval sculpture. The architect had had a plaster cast made of it when the cathedral was restored. It had been given as a token of respect. Only highly deserving scholars were presented with a copy when they lectured. Gunnar could not make me bat an eye.

There was silence around the oval table from Svenskt Tenn. Gunnar ate the rest of his cookie. His brother had nothing more to say. One of the relatives-by-marriage cleared his throat. I cast a blank look around the room. I showed no reaction. Gunnar leaned back in his armchair. He looked as if he were napping after his meal. But after a short while, he opened his eyes and peered out over the family. Then he looked straight at his brother and said:

"A certain inferior slag falls from every social class, doesn't it?"

And then he really fell asleep. While he leaned back, his head reclining against the armchair, snoring with his mouth open, the family sat with their coffee cups. They carefully took cookies and spoke quietly so as not to wake him.

I closed the encyclopedia and placed it by the telephone. Then I walked over to the table and took a ginger snap.

"So long," I said. "I'm going out awhile."

I turned then and went out the door, not looking back. I went down the stairs, leaving the relatives up there.

Gunnar hadn't succeeded on that occasion at Christmas, and he hadn't been able to get at me this time, either. I had managed on my own, and hadn't needed to ask for anyone's help.

The elevator boy opens the grating and I stand on the eleventh floor. My feet are a little sore, but I'll never admit it to anyone.

Night is falling swiftly now. After eating, I stand in the dark living room close to the window and look out over the Hudson River. The sky is clear. There, high over New Jersey, I see the navigation lights of a westbound night plane.

"They're flying to Chicago," I say.

Down there toward the water, streetlights shine. It's a long way to the far side of the river, and the advertising sign is lit. *THE TIME IS NOW 7:45.*

I feel a slight scratching in my hand, where I hold the turtle. It has begun to get used to me. It has its head and legs out and looks around with quick, jerky movements of its head. I rub its shell with my thumb. When it calms down still more, I will rub off the decal. I turn and walk down the corridor to my room.

Back in my room, I set up a little box for my turtle. The box is to stay under my bed. That's where it's going to live. But the next morning, the box is empty. The little turtle is gone. I look everywhere for it, but it is nowhere to be found. It's not until several months later that Karna finds it, while cleaning the apartment for Christmas. It got out of its box that night, crawled under the bookshelf and up on the ledge behind it. There it dried up and died. The decal proved that it was my turtle and not one stuck there from the time of the other boy (the one whose books were up in the cupboard).

The night after Karna found the dead, dehydrated turtle, after she showed it to me and we had thrown it in the trash and the trash had been carried out, that night I wake up and hear the garbage trucks far below, as they empty the trash can. Suddenly I feel very frightened and call out, loud enough to be heard:

"But just think if it wasn't really dead! Just think if it was only hibernating."

CHAPTER 12

On Wednesday afternoon I bought some magazines and a thick candy bar with a chewy filling at the German's shop. He had a little store selling newspapers and magazines, just around the corner on Broadway. It wasn't a real store, more like a hole in the wall, a cubbyhole. He also sold sweets—candy —from a glass-topped counter. That was the last time I ever went there.

Actually, I had planned to go to the drugstore next door. I had intended to seat myself on one of the high stools at the counter and order a strawberry ice cream soda. It had rained that night, but now the large clouds were gone. High up, the cirrus clouds moved swiftly across the sky towards the east. The wind had picked up and the green awning over the delicatessen flapped as I walked by, already seeing myself with the strawberry ice cream soda in front of me. But when I turned onto Broadway and got to the drugstore, I didn't go in. I peered through the door and then continued on up the street with the wind at my back. Standing inside were two 15-year-old boys. They leaned against the counter, with their left feet resting on the brass rail, as if they were standing at a real bar. They drank Coca-Cola through a straw. These were not natural straws, but the kind manufactured out of some sort of waxed paper. This I knew because I had already been in there once with Karna. We had ordered ice cream sodas and got straws like that. One of the boys now looked up, just as I reached the door. He looked right at me. I remember he had freckles. I could already hear myself ordering the soda, knew the boys would look at each other when they heard my accent. That's why I didn't enter the drugstore, even though I had been thinking about the strawberry ice cream soda as I walked in the wind all the way from Riverside Drive, and I had the money.

I had my first ice cream soda on board the *Kungsholm* on the way over. After that, I ordered it every chance I got. It was the best thing I had ever tasted. There was a combination of flavors that filled your whole mouth when you sucked it up the straw. It was the contrast between the salty soda water and the sweet ice cream. The thick stuff at the bottom you ate last with a long spoon. But I imagined the boys standing next to me, sneering, and I knew that the soda wouldn't taste that great. They would make comments about me. I would look straight ahead, and rush to finish and get out of there. That's why I didn't bother to go in.

I walked another block downtown, and the wind blew. Then after crossing 114th Street, I suddenly snapped my fingers, snorted and clapped my hands together, acting as though I had forgotten something important. By doing this I could turn around and go back the way I had come, without anyone wondering. As I passed the drugstore on my way back, I didn't even glimpse inside. I looked straight ahead and wrinkled my brow a little, as if deep in thought. There was no way I could go in now, even if the boys had gone. The man behind the counter might well have seen me hesitate the last time, and he might snigger when he recognized me now. Instead, I went into the German's shop at the corner. I called him "the German" because he didn't speak English properly. The words he used were generally correct (even though they were needlessly eloquent), but he pronounced them wrong. Because of this I was sure everyone could hear he was an immigrant, fresh off the boat. He couldn't manage the "W" or pronounce "TH" properly. Nor could he keep his voice clear and steady. It went up and down, and the words were spoken at different speeds, as in Europe. He also looked German. He was middle-aged, fat and bald, and he had small gold-rimmed glasses. He wore a dark suit with a horizontally striped tie, and a tie clip which might have been gold.

As I entered, he was busy counting the day's takings. He

divided the coins into small bags. He was not alone behind the counter; a woman also stood there. She, too, was middle-aged and fat. Her black hair was done in a knot and she wore a black dress of some shiny material. It was held together at the neck by a big silver brooch with a red gem in the middle. She was almost certainly the German's wife. The German, who was busy counting the receipts, looked up when I entered. I greeted them and then stood awhile at the magazine rack making my selection. There were many interesting magazines about science and such. Naturally, there were also film magazines, but they didn't interest me. And I couldn't buy the ones with pictures of girls clad in scanty bathing suits without them looking at me and saying something. I did sneak a look at the girls when I had my back to the German and his wife. I bought *Popular Science,* and then *Astounding.* After that, I carefully chose my candy. I finally decided on a Milky Way. I handed the wife a dollar bill and got back my change. After paying and saying thank you, I was about to go, when she clapped her hands together and said to her husband:

"Oh, what a polite, well-mannered European boy!"

Then I realized that I had bowed to them. The German stopped counting the money, pushed his glasses up on his head and looked at me.

"European boys are much nicer than Americans," she said.

"Yes," said the German. "He's been here before. He always bows."

"People are so impolite here in America," she said.

The German looked at me. We were alone in the little shop. He leaned forward and addressed me in a low voice.

"We appreciate that you bow when you come in. We were taught that boys should do that when they speak to their elders. But no one else bows. Here in America, people are always impolite, especially to old people and immigrants. And for that very reason, you should stop doing it. If you continue being polite, you'll never become an American and you'll have a hard time over here. We know you want to bow and that's enough. If you bow here you'll be very conspicuous. Everyone will see that you're a foreigner, and you'll be treated badly. You'll have a rough time. You've just arrived and you're only a child, so you can change."

"They overcharge you if they see you're an immigrant. And if they hear that you don't speak their language perfectly, they'll shortchange you and laugh and shove you away when you protest," the wife added.

"It's hard for an adult to change," said the German.

He was speaking rapidly now, and he began to gesticulate with his hands. He wore a thick gold wedding band on his right-hand ring finger. In Sweden and America, men wore their wedding ring on their left hand. If he didn't want to stick out here, he should shift his ring from one hand to the other, and he should stop waving his hands when he talked.

"A man is not an animal that changes color with the seasons. My wife and I, who were over 50 when we came here three years ago, have had to learn that there's no way pretending to be something we aren't. It's too late for us to learn to be different. But you should be on your guard. There's no mercy here. People here are like wolves; they don't laugh, they just show their teeth."

"That's right," added the wife. "Here in America you live like a wolf among wolves. The only way to survive is to howl with the pack."

"To forget is not as hard as *verlern*," said the German, laughing a little, as if he had made a joke.

I remained standing there with the change in my hand. The wife looked at the magazines I held under my arm. Then she bent down and took a magazine with a torn cover from off a stack behind the counter.

"Take this one, too, if you like," she said smiling.

"Otherwise, we would just have to return it," she said to her husband.

She held out the magazine with the torn cover and the German nodded kindly. As I took the magazine from her, he gestured to indicate that it was a present. He held out both his hand, palms up. They had given me last month's *Astounding,* the September issue.

Then he said:

"Please forgive us for speaking this way. People don't talk to children like this in America. They don't talk to them about life. They don't teach them anything. Here people allow the children to remain ignorant, to do whatever they like, to run wild. But then, when they grow up, all of a sudden they can only do or think what everyone else is doing or thinking. In Europe, we raised our children properly, so they would become real adults, with a conscience of their own."

I found it extremely unpleasant to stand here in this dingy, little shop and be lectured. It was like when I was at Ålsten School. Their eyes gleamed when they talked. The pupils looking at me were big and black. My spine tingled and I wanted to flee, wanted to get away from their looks and burst our and run away. But I stayed there with my magazines under my arm and change in my hand and looked at them and didn't know how I would be able to get away. They were both very emotional now. They spoke at the same time, and the wife interrupted her husband to say:

"But we mean well. You're from Europe and we know just how dangerous it is to make a mistake, to act like one does in Europe while here in America. We weren't accustomed to life here. Back home our lives were totally different. There we had a large store on Leipziger Strasse, and we had a house in Charlottenburg. But all that is gone now. That's how it goes! Now we must be glad that we have come here to America, and that we have a roof over our heads. Others have suffered more. But if you are going to get along here in America, you must not only talk like an American, you must also learn to be unfeeling and rude like an American, too. We know that now."

But they didn't look like the kind of people who had owned a place as big as Macy's huge department store down on 34th Street. I have been there. It is much bigger than Nordiska Kompaniet in Stockholm. Macy's is the world's largest department store. They couldn't have owned one that big. Not even one as big as NK. They look ordinary. They looked like the man who had the cigar store near Allé Park and his wife, who used to wear a sweater even in the summer. They were exaggerating, trying to make themselves something they were not. And if they had tried to tell people here about their big department store on Leipziger Strasse, I well understood why no one bothered to listen to them in America.

The wife had stopped talking. They both fell silent a moment. They looked at me, as if waiting for me to say something. I quickly said good-bye once more. Before they got a chance to start talking again, to say something more, I bowed, opened the door and walked out into the light of the street. Never again would I go there!

On the street, the wind was blowing harder than before. It now blew from down Broadway in sudden gusts. People were on their way up the street toward the subway station. A hatless woman walked in front of me. Her hair was dark, short and straight, and she was quite petite. From behind, I could see that she was young. She couldn't have been much more than twenty. Suddenly the wind hit her and sent her skirt billowing. Everyone looked at her. She held down the skirt in front with both hands, only to have the wind lift it in back, revealing a pair of small blue panties. She spun around and pulled in her skirt, holding it in a steady grip. She had bangs and a full mouth with red lips. She seemed almost angry as I looked her in the face. The men who had watched held onto their hats. They bent into the wind. Their raincoats flapped behind them, like great tails, as they struggled along behind her. A real storm was blowing now, and paper and litter came flying down the sidewalk toward me.

Outside the delicatessen, the awning had been torn from its iron frame in one corner, and it struck the wall with loud snapping sounds. A fat man in a white apron came out of the shop just as I walked by. He grabbed the rope dangling from the awning. It was clear that he was trying to fold it up. He pulled at it, but the awning swelled like a balloon. Little by little, it pulled loose from its frame, with small loud flaps and the man stood on his toes like a dancer as he hung onto the rope. Then the wind calmed and the awning fell back again. The man drew in the rope and stretched out his left hand, reaching for the canvas. But he had only just begun to pull it when the green material yanked out of his hand and flew up against the wall again, causing him to lose hold of the rope. There was a noise like a gunshot, and I saw the material torn apart. It began as a small rip at the edge and soon the awning had been ripped in two. The rope now hung limp. The fat man grabbed it, but it was already too late. A newspaper whirled by and the man, who still clung to the rope, looked stupid. He stepped aside to let people pass on the sidewalk. Above his head, the strips of awning flapped feebly in the wind which had now suddenly abated.

By the time I got to the north side of 116th Street and began walking down Riverside Drive, the wind had stopped blowing. And then without warning, it began again. It placed itself like a wall before me, and it was so dense that I could barely push my way through it. Down in the park, the trees bent and bowed to me. The air was thick with yellow dust. Leaves and branches came swirling toward my face. Small cartons, torn bags and what appeared to be old kitchen garbage flew along the walls of the buildings and got tangled up in my legs. I had to make a real effort not to be carried up toward Broadway by the wind. A loud crashing sound could be heard as the big garbage can down at the corner fell over and began to roll up the street in my direction. The lid danced in the wind and flew by. The can bounced and banged and thundered along against the asphalt, up toward Columbia University. That's going to end up in Morningside Park, I said to myself. There was no one else on the street, and very little traffic on Riverside Drive.

Entering the apartment building, the doorman said:

"They say on the radio that the storm got off course and, instead of hitting Florida, smashed into New England with winds reaching 60 miles an hour. It's a real hurricane."

That afternoon, I began to read *Astounding*. It was the first time I had seen the expression *science fiction* in the title of a magazine article. But these were the kind of stories that Jules Verne and H.G. Wells wrote. Stories like *The Time Machine* and *Engineer Robur's Air Voyage*. I had begun by lying on the floor, as usual. It was easier to read lying on the floor. That way I could have my books and magazines spread out around me. They were all there, face down, within easy reach. I could go from one book to the other in my reading, just as I wished, without worrying about having books shut accidentally and losing my place. If I sat in an armchair with my books stacked on a table, it always took me a little time to find where I was. I often had to leaf through the book, searching. Tables were never big enough to accommodate all the books I had going, so I couldn't leave them open. But now, spread in front of me, I had only the three magazines and two of the books I had found up in the cupboard and had taken down that morning. One was a thick volume, 1152 pages of close print, with a green cover. It was quite tattered and the title was *A Century of Creepy Stories*. It appeared to be full of interesting ghost stories. The other book was an illustrated edition of *Alice in Wonderland*. In the illustrations, this Alice was neither old-fashioned nor childish. She was drawn as a very pretty girl, with dark hair cut in a pageboy, slightly slanting eyes and half-open mouth. She wore low-heeled black pumps, white stockings and a short checked skirt. When Alice fell down the rabbit hole, the skirt ought to have flown higher than the little bit shown in the picture. She had fallen very slowly, of course. She smiled a little and closed her eyes as she fell. I wondered how she could see the cards and everything that was on the walls around her as she fell. She should have had her eyes open. Actually, I didn't care for illustrated books. I preferred to create my own images as I read. That way there wasn't such a discrepancy between words and pictures. But this particular Alice I looked at, even though I had read the story many times. I laid it aside opened to the page where Alice stands rather shyly in the Duchess' kitchen, while the cat grins. That was a picture to reflect on. Then I went back to the *Astounding* story of the robots who come to earth and realize that the strange, primitive earth protoplasm is alive, in its own way, and that they themselves derive their origin from just such earthly protoplasmic life. They themselves are descended from beings who achieved the beginnings of consciousness, enabling them to create life by bringing into being the first thinking mechanical creatures in the distant past.

The wind whistled through the window. It wouldn't shut tight. The heavy brown curtains swelled with the draft from behind and the wooden rings rattled along the curtain rod. The curtains jerked and tugged. Then they fell back and I could feel the draft along the floor. The wind began to blow again. It shook the window and blew through the gaps around the window. From time to time, I felt the chill run up my spine and neck. And even though I had closed the door and remained perfectly still, I heard how the wind shook the doors as the curtains billowed and fell.

I began to feel cold in the draft. I considered moving up onto my bed with the magazines and books. There was room there next to the radio. This was an American model, with only a medium wave band. Here in America, people only listened to medium wave. But there were many stations in New York. This particular radio featured six push buttons for different stations. The boy who had lived here before me had set them.

I stacked the magazines and books on the bed next to the radio. I switched on the radio and watched the light come on behind the glass, where all the wave lengths were shown. I pushed the button for station WABC, broadcasting at 860 kilocycles. It took a while for the radio to warm up. The announcer said that Xavier Cugat *and his famous orchestra* would be playing *dinner-dance music* from the Sert Room at the Waldorf Astoria. I left it on low, in case something interesting came on; in any case, the music didn't bother me.

Before I took up my reading again, I went out to Karna in the kitchen and asked for a snack. We wouldn't be eating for a couple of hours. She was busy making a real American apple pie. At first she said that I didn't need a snack. Then she relented. She prepared a small tray that I could take into my room. On a round brass tray, she placed two ice-cold bottles of Coca-Cola, two straws, a bottle opener and a blue glass bowl of saltine crackers. These crackers were small, round and salty American biscuits called *Ritz*. Alva and Gunnar had them with their afternoon cocktails. They sat in the living room, each on a yellow sofa, in front of the artificial fire, with the glass table between them. They read newspapers and sipped their drinks and on the table were bowls of salt crackers, olives and salted peanuts and a white porcelain platter that looked like a giant grape leaf with small appetizers like pieces of cheese and things. In addition, Gunnar had a large ashtray by him. He smoked two packs a day. Just now he mainly smoked *Camels*. He also mixed the drinks himself, pouring the gin, vermouth and ice in the glass and stainless steel shaker. He said he made them himself because he wanted them drier.

I carried the tray into my room. I made a place for it next to the radio. I kept the music low and sat with my legs crossed on the bed. I had opened a bottle of Coca Cola and drank it through a straw, as I read on in the *Astounding* with the torn cover about the robots' emotions when they learned of their shameful origins. The whole time, Xavier Cugat and his famous orchestra played on the radio by my side. From time to time, I reached out and took a cracker, released the straw, and put the crisp, salty, slightly greasy cracker in my mouth and chewed it. Then I sucked slowly on the straw so that the good cola taste would last longer. When the first bottle was finished and there was just a little gurgling down at the bottom when I drew on the straw, I opened the second bottle and continued drinking.

You could also imagine the story of the robots the other way around. It could be that mankind's obscure urge (yes, I would have used the phrase "mankinds obscure urge" if I had written the story) to build and surround itself with ever more complicated machines was a hereditary characteristic, with which the protoplasm had been equipped from the beginning. This was its very purpose in life. It just might be that machines were the first inhabitants of the universe. They were more viable than the protoplasm. They didn't require any special oxygenized atmosphere, air pressure or special temperature. And they were not as short-lived and self-destructive as protoplasm. Several million protoplasmic years ago (equivalent to only a few machine-days), the machines had set up a small laboratory on earth, a workshop where interested machines experimented with a new, special method for the design and production of machinery.

The most intricate small adjustments and polishing was best done by protoplasmic implements. In addition, oils were initially protoplasmic by nature, and if the oil became active, it had superior lubrication capability. This had been known for several machine-centuries. The question was, however, whether this implement could be so precisely adjusted that it could be utilized

for the design of new machinery. To determine this, a protein
gruel was prepared. It was poured into a solution of tepid, salty
H_2O, in shallow stone containers, where it dissolved and was radi-
ated with ultraviolet rays until it began to stir and live. But this
time, instead of immediately using this self-pulsating mass for polish and lubrication, as was the custom, embryos were put in the
gruel and the protoplasm was allowed to develop, to build cells,
to evolve from one cell to many, and then, completely according
to plan and to pre-determined genetic engineering, to go from
one species to the next, until the human implement, with eyes,
brain and opposable thumb was complete and only needed several thousand years of fine tuning to arrive at the point where it
could produce machines. It might have been like that. We might
actually be machines invented by machines. When our cars
wouldn't start, it was perhaps out of a primeval (primeval because
the earthly cars, with their combustion motors for fossil protoplasm, were extremely primitive and embryonic machines) feeling
that it was degrading for a machine to serve a protoplasmic being.

I put *Astounding* aside and sat thinking about this. On the
radio, the announcer now said the hurricane had struck a town on
Buzzards Bay, Massachusetts, so hard that a man almost drowned
in the center of the town square. When the storm struck, he went
to get a little girl who had been left in a car in the square. As he
went to rescue her, he was able to walk all the way to the car
without getting wet. But carrying her back, a flood of water struck
the town. He had to wade through water that rose to his chin, and
he almost drowned. They were both saved, however, by neighbors, who threw a fire rescue line from the window of the mayor's
office. He was able to haul himself and the girl up onto the steps
of the city hall. According to the radio, they were all still up on
the roof of the city hall waiting to be rescued. Then it was back to
Xavier Cugat.

I spun out the story of the protoplasmic implements in various directions. But it was hard to get it to jibe. There were big holes in it. I tried to fix it by writing myself into the story. I could just go out the door, where the wind had blown such a gap in reality that I might suddenly pass though the wall into the world of machines, right into the laboratory . . . There I looked through the microscope observing humanity and then looked up at the thinking machines that had created us. Thus, I became the first protoplasmic being to understand the true situation. But this story wouldn't work either. It was full of holes too. Gaps that couldn't be explained without a drawn-out account. I stopped making up stories. The bottles, too, were empty.

The announcer on the radio said that the seismological instruments at Fordham University in New York had been registering increasingly intense microseismic tremors since one p.m. These microseismic tremors occur when floods caused by storms hammer the continental coastline at the same time as the land mass is subjected to sudden changes in air pressure, Professor Martin F. Bradford explained to the announcer in reply to his question. It was the hurricane over New England that was stirring up things in New York, he said. Then Xavier Cugat and his orchestra came on again.

Even though we were really only at the edge of the storm, I sat on my bed and tried to feel all Manhattan shaking. But all I heard was the wind. I couldn't feel any subterranean tremors. I recognized that Xavier Cugat and his orchestra were playing rumbas. And I was alone in my room, so I took out the book about Alice again. There was a picture in it that occasionally popped up in my mind, a picture I had just thought of, as I fantasized about the world of machines. I wanted to take a good long look at it now. It was the one where she sat in court next to the doormouse and grew tall without being able to do anything about it.

It was toward the end of the book. My throat was already a little dry. When I reached for the book, I knew what I was going to do. I opened the book and placed it beside me. I sat with my legs crossed next to it and looked. Alice sat on the bench. It had already become far too small for her. She looked down at the doormouse to her left. She had drawn up her legs, holding them tightly to her. Her rounded knees were bare, since the white stockings were short and her skirt had traveled high up her thigh. In the drawing you could also see a glimpse of what must have been the hem of her underwear in the shadow beneath her left thigh. I removed the doormouse. I wanted Alice to be alone in the picture. Then I had her look up, right at me. Then I began to spread her legs. At first she resisted, holding them shut. The skirt slid higher. I saw the inside of her right thigh. But I didn't want her checked skirt to ride too high at once. She kept her hands on her knees. Now she put her palms down on the bench, leaned back, looking at me, and began to part her legs. At first, I thought I'd have her wear panties, but then I imagined her without. I wanted to see her naked under her skirt. I let her drop her gaze again, as she spread her legs wider and wider. She spread her thighs and the checked skirt almost reached her waist. My heart was beating violently now. Alice closed her eyes and leaned her head back, extending her throat and letting her straight dark hair hang free. She had come out of the picture now; she was there before me. I heard her breathing. Her mouth was open. I saw my hands grab her knees. I felt the warm, smooth skin with the tips of my fingers, there on the inside of her thigh. My mouth was dry. I felt the blood pulse in my neck and at the back of my eyes. Then I stopped. It would soon be dinnertime, and without warning someone might walk into the room. I put Alice away. But my heart was still beating so violently that I felt a pain in my chest.

I shut the book. On the radio, the announcer now said the wind was blowing 120 miles an hour at the meteorological station on top of the Empire State Building. But while listening to the announcer, I realized that I wanted to see Alice this way one more time, and I opened the book again, turned to the picture of her falling down the rabbit hole, and I looked at it. Actually, I preferred this picture. She had her mouth open and her smile was nicer here. Alice also held her arms above her head in this picture. I now blew the skirt up so she was naked all the way up to her navel. Her checked skirt was so short that it didn't conceal her face. And there she was, still smiling, holding her arms above her head, while her dark hair streamed in the wind. Alice should have been naked in this picture. I wanted to see her naked. Her cunt, too, I thought. But I let Alice keep her eyes closed, let her move her legs very slowly while falling, as if she were languidly dancing for me in a movie. As if I had Alice filmed in slow motion while she was falling and the movie was then shown for me. I was breathing very heavily, sitting there on the bed with my legs crossed, looking at Alice. Then I quickly closed the book and put it away behind the radio. I wanted to hide it so no one would find it.

Actually, this was unnecessary. It didn't matter who found the book and looked through it. It didn't matter. There was nothing there to see. No one would understand the way I had looked at it. I didn't know if other people could look at a picture like that, whether they could change what they saw as they wished. I didn't think so. They talked like they didn't see the pictures. They weren't able to lift the picture from the page and make it come alive. And I was careful not to tell about the pictures, about how you could go about seeing things, and how you could change what you saw. They just wouldn't understand.

This was the first book I saw in which Alice was drawn in a way that made me want to take the picture, look at her and do these things to her. In children's books, girls were almost never drawn so that one could really see or look at them. But here in this picture, Alice was drawn in such a way that she appeared to actually exist beneath her clothes, as though she could step out of the picture and into the room. And yet, there was nothing tangibly different in these pictures, nothing to distinguish them from those in other children's books. It wasn't as though she were undressed, or anything. Perhaps it was a certain expression on her lips, or the way she squinted or walked in the pictures. But she stood in a special way in the duchess' kitchen, and she let herself fall through the well in a certain way, and she drew up her legs and held her knees together in a certain way in the picture where she sat with the doormouse. I had noticed it the minute I first browsed through the book. The man who illustrated the book must have known. But I didn't believe that anyone else would notice.

I had taken the books out that morning. I had climbed up on the chair and opened the upper cupboard in the closet, where the boy who had lived here before me had stored his books. There were a number of storybooks, including *The Wizard of Oz* and others of the Oz series. There were detective stories by Freeman Wills Crofts, Agatha Christie, Ellery Queen and others. There were adventure stories of various types and the tattered volume of creepy stories, which I took out and put aside as soon as I saw it, intending to read it that very day. There were school books and many others, and there was the illustrated *Alice in Wonderland*. I had not had the slightest intention of getting it down. I had already read the story and knew it well; but in any case, I picked up the book to move it aside, opened it at random and found the picture where Alice stands in the Duchess' kitchen. Something clicked inside, the blood rushed to my face, I felt my heart beat, and, although I knew no one was there, I had to look around to make sure I was alone in the room and that no one was looking.

I stood still a moment, looking at the picture. The Duchess and the cook were ugly, and the kitchen was full of smoke. The child screamed and the cat grinned down in the right-hand corner. But Alice was both there in the room and somewhere else at the same time. It was as though she took no notice of the smoke and noise. She stood in front of the smoke. Alice wore a short checked skirt, a simple, straight blouse with short sleeves and a white collar. She stood with her hands behind her back, so that her hips were pushed slightly forward and emphasized. She looked down at the floor and I couldn't see her eyes. She smiled a little. Her dark hair was drawn with a different luster from that of the others in the background of the picture. She stood at ease, but with a tenseness beneath her clothing, as if she were waiting for something to happen. Her weight rested on the left leg. She bent her right leg slightly and her foot was forward and turned aside. I could see her thigh muscle tense. I couldn't stand there on the chair like that, so I quickly closed the book and laid it aside. I pushed it under the volume of horror stories. That way no one would see it. I wanted it for myself. I knew that I would look at the pictures of Alice later that afternoon. The sun was now shining outside and a great swatch of sunlight lay on the floor, and I was going out after lunch. I wanted an ice cream soda.

They were talking about the hurricane on the radio again. At the Blue Hill Observatory outside Boston, the instruments had registered a wind velocity of 186 miles an hour before they were destroyed by the wind. The announcer was interviewing the head of the observatory. Dr. C.F. Brooks said that the wind was now coming in great, heavy gusts. Each gust pushed the wind velocity to 120 miles an hour. These gusts lasted up to five minutes each. From the observatory they could hear when the gusts of wind came. First an infernal noise was heard from the bowels of the earth. Then came the great wind. But in the end, the wind grew so violent that all the instruments were destroyed, after a final registration of 186 miles an hour. The speaker thanked the doctor and said that we would now return to Xavier Cugat and his famous orchestra, who were playing rumba rhythms from the dance floor of the Sert Room at the Waldorf Astoria.

It was difficult to hear what the head of the observatory had said. All the telephone and power lines in New England had blown down. He was talking on one of the Navy's emergency transmitters. Then the music came back on and I told myself: now I erase Alice from my mind. I haven't seen her. I won't let the images come back. Now no one can look at me and see what I've been thinking. Just then the announcer interrupted the broadcast from the Waldorf Astoria to say that the meteorologist Professor Kirby had just arrived at the studio. He would explain the cause of the floods which had hit the northeastern states. The professor said the floods were particularly heavy due to the gravitational pull of the sun and moon on the tides. The moon was now in its position closest to the earth, and the tides were a foot higher than normal. In addition to this there was the volume of water the hurricane pushed before it on its way across the Atlantic. When this body of water neared the shallow coastal water, it was forced to rise in a high wall of water that crashed down over the land.

Just then I heard Karna calling me. Dinner was ready. I turned off the radio and went into the kitchen to eat. There was apple pie with cream for dessert.

"The wind is awful today," she said.

I began to tell her about the winds over the Atlantic, about the air pressure and the influence of the moon on the flood, but she had no time to listen to me. She was in a hurry. She was going to International House to dance.

That evening, I lay a long time reading *Creepy Stories*. First I read about a girl whose dead cousin became her best friend and playmate. Eventually, the dead cousin enticed the girl to join her in death. Her motive was revenge. It seems the girl's father had allowed the cousin to burn to death so he could inherit the wealth of his brother. I had to find another radio station in the middle of the story because WABC was broadcasting a silly romantic comedy about a girl who went out on various dates and had an insufferable little brother. I tried different radio stations, looking for something to listen to while I read. They were mostly offering concerts by squeaky string bands, piano music and tenors. There were stories about families who experienced various things, but no matter what they did, they were still good-hearted souls inside. Finally I was able to find a station playing music I could listen to while reading. The yodeling brakeman sang about how he traveled the country, picking apples in Tennessee, peaches in Georgia and girls in Alabama.

"Then it's girl pickin' time for me," he sang, while he played Hawaiian music on his guitar. And then he yodeled a little and sang some more.

Afterward they talked a little about him. His name was Jimmy Rodgers and he was dead. Then they played more of his songs, while I read about Elspeth Clewer. She was buried in 1572, but lay restless in her grave. She sent her spiteful spirit back into the world of the living, where she entered the soul of a young woman in England ten years ago. The man who loved this girl had to bury her in a lead coffin, put a stake through her heart and slit the tendons of her heels, so she wouldn't become a ghost again. While I was reading this story, they were telling more about Rodgers on the radio. He played the guitar, yodeled and sang a little about how this girl was waiting for him on Saturday night to get her hands on his paycheck.

By then I had begun the story about the man, one of the undead, who lay several hundred years in an inn. He had risen up beneath his shroud when the professor, who had come to write about the Roman Empire in peace and quiet, out of curiosity tried all the keys in the lock to get into the sealed room. This story really was scary and I saw my curtains swell in the wind. I put the book aside. There was more news about the hurricane on the radio. But on this station, the news was presented from a different angle. The announcer strummed a guitar while speaking of the hurricane. He told about a man in New Hampshire who had seen

Ocean-born Mary return to Concord in a four-horse carriage. It was her custom to return in October, but now she had come as an omen. He saw her out on the pier, the wind tearing at her full, gray, ghostly skirts. When he approached, she waved as if warding him off, and he realized that something was about to happen. Just then he saw a thick gray mist rolling in over the ocean. He remembered her warning in time, however, and understood that it wasn't a fogbank, but a gigantic wall of wind-whipped water. He ran away and escaped the hurricane. But if it hadn't been for Ocean-born Mary's warning, he would have been swept away and drowned. The speaker told this in a sort of dry voice, with a slightly rolling rhythm, while strumming the guitar. Then he said that we shouldn't wait for an omen, since God was calling each and every one of us this very day. And the man on the pier was like you or me before the sea of sin that would drown everyone on its day of wrath. The figure on the pier had been none other than Jesus Christ. I understood then that this was no newsman and that I had tuned into a sermon. I turned it off.

I must have fallen asleep immediately, for when I woke up the next morning, the lights in the room were still on. I turned on the radio and listened to the morning news on WABC. The announcer said that 480 people had died the previous afternoon and night in the hurricane, which had also felled 250 million trees in New England and ruined the maple-syrup industry for a generation to come.

CHAPTER 13

The school I now attended was built of red brick, darkened with age. Its facilities were old, its address unfashionable. It lay on the far side of Columbia University, on the other side of the park, right by Harlem, the Negro section and immigrant slum. But the school was so liberal and famous that the address made no difference.

I walk up the avenue. It is late October 1938. Further on, to my right, I see the park. I cross the street, turn right and am now about to enter the school to my left, through the door of 425 West 123rd Street, just north of Morningside Park at Amsterdam Avenue. This is my school. Lincoln School. What, then, do I know about it, after one month?

It is progressive, an experimental school and laboratory for the Teachers College at Columbia University. This is where model curricula and school systems are developed for the whole world, for the dawning, glorious age of Democracy. Our teachers are the most gifted assistants to the time's most brilliant, world-famous professors of education, at the world's greatest university. All of us who go here are gifted. We are tested and are subject to continual monitoring. I don't think anyone is admitted without a minimum IQ of 120, according to Terman-Merrill. Most of us belong to the 8th percentile with an IQ of over 125. But those of us among the 2% gifted, with higher or much higher IQs, are difficult to place. The intelligence tests actually only work for the lower 92%; the children who are just normal and those slightly below. If they aren't from the slums, children like these generally go to newer, nicer schools in better neighborhoods. They cram. They don't study independently like we do. And for us, there's no need for new buildings and modern facilities.

But we are without prejudice. Everybody is just as good as everybody else. Even those of average and below average intelligence, even those who attend schools in the slums, are as good as we are. This is one of our school's great traditions. *All men are created equal.* The school upholds the democratic ideals. Neither race, religion or place of origin shall be grounds for discrimination among citizens with equal rights in a free republic. The only difference between the other 92% and ourselves is that we are more intelligent. That is why we don't have to cram; we can study as we like and develop our natural aptitudes. However, those of us who attend this school have one other thing in common, besides intelligence. We all come from the same background. Our parents are all intellectuals. We know it without having to talk about it all the time. It's obvious. We all belong.

I know that many of my fellow pupils have parents who are divorced and remarried, some of them several times. This can lead to extremely complicated family relations, with several sets of siblings and half-siblings, siblings by marriage in various degrees. But it is always the same sort of parent, no matter how many times they remarry. All of a sudden, one's schoolmate has changed fathers again. The new one is not a professor, he's an advertising executive. We never speak of it. We just don't. You must always be careful, however, since you never know who is father to whom or how your schoolmate is related to his mother, sister, or brothers.

Some of the fathers are professors at the university, others are liberal bankers from the great banking firms. Some of them have been loaned out to the government by the university or banks, to administer Roosevelt's *New Deal* down in Washington. Other fathers are publishers, editors, columnists, and correspondents for the major newspapers. Some are radio executives. Some are in advertising. There are architects, and liberal rabbis, theologians and broad-minded, high-ranking Protestant clergymen. The only politician with a child enrolled in the school is the leader of the Socialist Party. But he isn't a politician like the others. He is an intellectual and doesn't involve himself in the usual political deals, worked out in smoke-filled rooms. I know of no regular business-men, butchers, drugstore owners, wholesalers, small entrepre-neurs, or people like bookkeepers, salesmen, and the like, among the fathers of my classmates. But if there were someone whose father had such an occupation, perhaps he would just keep it to himself. This, too, is a subject we avoid. There are also some European refugees here. Their fathers are professors or artists.

Gunnar has been summoned to America by the Carnegie Corporation of New York to direct a comprehensive, objective and dispassionate study of the Negro in America as a social phenome-non. People know this and they approve. After all, there is no racial prejudice at the school.

Still, I can't recall there being any black pupils there. Perhaps I just didn't notice them.

With few exceptions, the mothers are well educated and intel-lectually inclined. They have servants so they can take an active part in social and community affairs. They are interested in litera-ture and the theater, as well as issues of social equality, psycholo-gy and child rearing. Some of them also work outside the home. They are leaders of women's professional organizations. Alva is studying at the university. She is a psychologist, like so many of the mothers.

We learn to sing gospel songs and listen to revivalist songs from the South, since this is part of the curriculum in Folklore, Folkways and the American Heritage. But we never discuss our own religions. This isn't done. This is a liberal school, so there are both Jews and Catholics attending. I myself am an atheist. But I never have to explain or defend my beliefs. I don't know if any of us goes to church or synagogue. Here in America the church is completely separate from school. We are not Jewish, Greek, Italian or Swedish here. We are Americans and speak English. As for politics, we have regular class discussions about current events. We form opinions about social issues solely on rational grounds. Knowledge is essential for a sense of citizenship.

The question of unemployment is especially important and instructive at present. In this matter, Roosevelt has done a great deal to change the old view on governmental intervention. The President's signing of the Social Security Act on August 14, 1935, and the Supreme Court's decision of May 24, 1937, declaring the constitutionality of using tax revenues for social security, were red-letter days in contemporary history. Here in the state of New York, the State Employment Service had paid $66,689,661.16 to officially recognized unemployed workers, between January 1, 1938 (when the unemployed could first legally collect unemployment benefits from the money paid in by the employers since March 1936) and September 1, 1938. This they had us commit to memory. But unemployment still continues to rise. The teacher says that according to official statistics there were 9,918,000 people unemployed at the beginning of September, but the son of the leader of the Socialist Party says that the AF of L claims the actual number is 10,539,000. We have a very good and fruitful debate chaired by the teacher. He also raises the question of whether these benefits have reduced the willingness to work. For the most part, we believe that this has not been the case. It is only in the event that relief payments become too generous that this might become a danger. Doing away with the benefits, however, might lead to undesirable social consequences, such as an increase in crime.

There is also a political wall newspaper, where we report events in Europe and other parts of the world, and what the dictators are doing. We hold many different opinions, otherwise we wouldn't be able to talk things over and debate, we wouldn't learn to listen to an argument and refute it. Nor would we be able to elect representatives to the wall newspaper committee, responsible for reporting current events, or to the class and student councils, which manage our self-government. But we all agree about the New Deal. I can't recall a Republican among us. During our discussions, I have been asked about socialism. After all, I am from Europe. I point out that in Sweden, they are Democrats, even if they call themselves Social Democrats; it is something similar to our not just saying Democrat here in America, but specifying New Deal Democrat and Southern Democrat.

There are differences among us. Not all the families have the same income, wealth or status. Some of the students are members of the Sixty Families, while others are the children of low-paid teachers. Some live in enormous penthouses near Central Park and have their own chauffeurs, and others live right on the edge of Harlem, in some ordinary little apartment, in some old tenement building, without servants or even an elevator. You can't tell who is who by looking at the pupils or their clothing, for we are not supposed to act or dress in the English or European style, but like regular American boys. But the names are a giveaway. Those belonging to the Sixty Families have another sort of name; they include numerals. In Europe, it is only royalty who have such names, but here in America, royal privilege does not exist. Here, all the rich and old families have that kind of name.

For example, if I were not an immigrant, but a member of one of those families, I would have been named Karl Pettersson III. I would have been the third to bear the name of my paternal grandfather, who founded the family fortune through extensive speculation in wheat in Chicago, just before the turn of the century. Gunnar wouldn't have had to change his name from Pettersson to Myrdal. There were also those at school who indicated their succession not with Roman, but with Arabic numerals. That way my name would have been written Karl Pettersson 3rd. This was actually a little more elegant, since it indicated that I was the eldest son of the eldest son. If it were written with Roman numerals, it might mean that my paternal grandfather was a failure and that it was Grandpa's brother whose name was Karl Pettersson and who had made the fortune, when he emigrated to Willmar, Minnesota, and founded a bank. Arabic numerals indicated that there was an unbroken succession. I might also have been called Karl Gunnar Myrdal Jr. This was often done here in families where the father had made the fortune or become famous. In that case, however, Gunnar would have had to become famous in America before I was born. At school, there are only a handful with a junior after their name. All the children at school have a middle initial. They don't use unadorned names, consisting only of first and last name, like mine, Jan Myrdal. I would be the only one in my class without a middle initial.

"America is an old-fashioned Europe," Gunnar had said. "People here are of peasant stock. They had no family names when they came to America. That's why they all really have the same type of names as in Russia. That was how it used to be in Sweden too. You only had a name and then the patronymic, the father's name. Great-great-great-great grandfather had no family name as he was a peasant on Lövåsen. He was Danielsson after his father, and his name was Jöns and thus his son was Jönsson and his own name was Petter, and his son thus was Persson and his own name was Erik. But as his father had moved from Lövåsen when he married in 1752 and cleared new land, he belonged to Myres now and was called Myr Erik Persson. But even so Myr was no family name but the name of the famly land, and his son became Myr Erik Ersson and my grandfather thus was Petter Ersson, and Father then took the patronymic as a family name and became Carl Adolf Pettersson, and I followed in the new system as Karl Gunnar Pettersson and then took back the name Myr as Myrdal. But in Russia things took a different path. There the peasantry was not free; they had no family name and no farm name. They were like the Negroes in the American South, who didn't have their own names. They were named after their masters. That's why the Russians have now adopted the same sort of name as Count Tolstoy. Lev was his proper name, Nikolaievitch, his patronymic, and the famous Tolstoy, his last name. And it was as Tolstoy, he became known throughout the world. Here in America, the immigrants did the same thing. They got land, began to grow rich, and wanted to have real names. That's why one always has a first name, Charles, for instance; an initial, which serves as a patronymic, G, for instance; and the name they have adopted as a surname, Smith or something. Now that you're in America, you must have a real American name. So here you'll be known as Jan G. Myrdal, the G standing for Gunnar."

And so I received my new American name. Now no one could tell I was an immigrant just by looking at my name. I had a middle initial like everyone else. This change was made before I started school. No one had a chance to learn that I didn't have an initial.

However, we don't talk about his kind of thing at school. It's just not done. This is a democratic school and in America we do not judge by appearances. There are no inherited titles or nobility, as in Europe. It is part of our American heritage to respect the individuality of each person. If I were to start asking my schoolmates about their names, I would just be showing that I had recently arrived from Europe, where this business of names and families means something. That's why I don't let on that I am thinking about their names or that I am trying to figure out why one has a Jr. following his name, another has III, and still another 3rd.

And neither do we speak of our families' wealth. This is contrary to common belief in Europe, where they think that bragging and talking about one's money and religion is typically American behavior. In our school, at least, this is not the case. Perhaps they do that in other schools, but here in our school, we don't care who comes from an important family or who is rich or who comes almost from the slums. Everyone is equal no matter what. In this school we never speak of a family's religion or money. Nevertheless, I lie on the floor of my bedroom and read about the families of my extremely rich schoolmates, in Gustavus Meyer's *History of the Great American Fortunes*. It was during the Gilded Age, a century age that their great-grandfathers, maternal and paternal grandparents, made their names and came to be known as the robber barons. But nowadays, the only indication is the III and 3rd, and their address.

I don't remember my first day at Lincoln School. I can't recall how I got there or how I learned my way around the building. It's almost a complete blank. I just see myself seated in the testing room, trying to put together a mosaic of different colored wooden triangles and squares. This followed the traditional intelligence test. I sit there thinking a moment. Outside, the sun is shining on the dark brick walls, and I try to remember what I know about this kind of test, and what it well mean for me. Suddenly I'm attending school, one of the American pupils. The first thing I see, after having walked up the avenue, crossed the street and passed thoroughout the door of the old, sooty, red-brick building on 123rd Street, is myself standing in the classroom on the third floor, in front of the wall newspaper hanging from two large black iron hooks on the brick wall, directly to the right of the door. The wall newspaper is a board covered in gray cloth, inside a varnished yellow frame of wood. We post newspaper clippings there with thumbtacks. I am to be a member of the wall-newspaper commit-tee. We have cut out articles about the settlement in Munich. They'll give a day-by-day account of what is happening to Czechoslovakia. We will read them so that we will be able to dis-cuss the situation in Europe next week. I turn towards the boy with the horn-rimmed glasses. I believe he is Jewish and his father is in Washington, helping Roosevelt regulate the banks in some way. He is putting up a *New York Times* article reporting that Czechoslovakia's former president Benes, the man the French and English removed from office because Hitler demanded it, was now going to come teach at the University of Chicago. What remained of Czechoslovakia had been forced to change domestic policy and to become pro-German, and therefore could not permit him to remain in the country.

"Hitler is going to grab Prague, too," I say. "Chamberlain has been fooled."

"Yes, they're going to start another war over there in Europe," he says. "They think it'll be next spring or summer."

CHAPTER 14

It was right after lunch. She sat across the table from me, smiling. She was the school psychologist. At first they thought it was the language. Then they tried to talk to me. And finally, they sent me here. Someone had come into the classroom and told me to come along. We were in the middle of a math lesson and everyone looked at me when I got up and went out into the hall. It was the first time I visited her, although I remembered the room from the tests. She wore a white lab coat, unbuttoned. She had frizzy blond hair and blue eyes. When she smiled, she showed her teeth. She smiled the whole time, and I remembered what the German had said:

"Here in America, they grin when they smile."

But I thought this to myself and smiled back the whole time. I didn't show my teeth. I just let the smile remain fixed on my face, no matter what she said or what I was thinking. When I spoke to her, I also smiled.

She had the green file with my papers in it on her desk, as well as her notebook. It was black. In her pocket, above her left breast, she had two pens. When I entered the room, she said she was so glad to meet me. It was always difficult to begin a new school, she said, and especially hard to begin a new school in a new part of the world. She understood so well. But I smiled and assured her that I didn't find it difficult, that I liked it very much and that everything was fine at this school.

I knew why I had been sent here. I pretended I believed her when she said that she spoke to all the new pupils, so that they would get a good start. It had started the very first week, when I had been told to run with the others in the gym. I didn't move. I just said:

"I can't."

First they smiled and acted lively. But I just looked right through all of them and said:

"*I can't.*"

The ceiling was very high. The gymnasium was on the top floor. Up there the windows were filthy. It was obvious they were never washed, being so far off the floor. On that occasion, nothing else happened. I stood there a moment, and then was allowed to leave.

In the gym a few days later, they tried again. The same thing happened. I was supposed to play in a basketball game. I had changed into my gym clothes with all the others. There in the locker room, in from of the tall, gray, steel lockers, Theobald pretended he was a girl, as usual. He had shoved his penis back behind his thighs and strutted about, swaying his bottom and talking in a feminine voice. Everyone laughed. I laughed too. Theobald was quite fat. He was from Germany and lived over in New Jersey. You could tell by the way he spoke that he was not born here, but in Germany. I believe his father was a theologian.

It was Theobald who had told me one day at lunch not to use the word "heinie" as a curse, since it wasn't a swearword, but just a bad word for Germans. I had thought it meant ass, for the others had smacked themselves on the bottom and shouted "heinies." It smelled of sweat in the locker room, where Theobald now strutted about, and everyone was shouting and laughing. When we had changed, I left the locker room and walked into the large gym hall with all the others. But once there, I quietly placed myself by the high end wall. For I had looked out across the gym floor where we were to play, and I could see myself running and jumping for the ball, touching it with my fingers only to have it taken away. The others would run ahead and I would run behind. I would be as ridiculous as Theobald. I felt ashamed, as I pictured what would happen if I stepped out onto the playing floor. I felt so ashamed that I would have turned blood red if I had let anyone know what I was thinking. But I smiled, stood still, and didn't go into the room. I noticed that the floor was worn. It hadn't been varnished in a long time. The others jumped around and carried on. They were loosening up for the game. They shouted to one another.

"Come here, John," the coach called.

He wore a whistle on a string around his neck and he didn't walk across the floor, but jogged with his chin up. He bounced and threw his elbows about. I just said the same thing I had said when he had told me to run:

"*I can't.*"

I don't recall what he said to me then. I wasn't listening. In any case, I knew what they would say. They would always say the same thing. I just stood there and looked through them all. I didn't even lean against the brick wall. I looked at the others. Now they were playing the game, divided into two teams. They were competing. Some of them were good and others were clumsy. They looked like they were having fun. Theobald clowned around for them. He swayed his large behind and his stomach swished about when he made as if to take the ball. They hollered, jumped, screamed and reached for the ball.

Had they been kittens they would have jumped the same way if I had held a ball of yarn above their heads. They stamped on the floor. They ran. They yelled at each other all at the same time and jumped for the ball. I didn't move. I just stood where I was. Not even when Theobald threw the ball right at me, did I move. As the ball came at me I didn't even raise my hand. They all giggled when he threw it. They smiled, showing their front teeth. The ball hit me on the forehead and it would have hurt if I had allowed myself to feel it. As it was, I didn't bat an eye and the ball, which had struck me, fell to the floor and slowly rolled away. For one short moment they all stood still and looked at me. Then they picked up the ball again and began once more to run around with it, holler and gesticulate wildly.

It was in this room, I remembered, that they had tested me, when I was about to start at Lincoln School. It had been one of the office girls, dressed in a white blouse and black skirt, who had administered the test—or so I had thought at first. It was the standard Terman-Merrill test, only in English. I had thought to myself that she wasn't very superior or even gifted. But she was a nice girl, and I knew just about where I should be on the scale. Later, she had placed the colored counters on a tray for me and had asked me to arrange them. And then I realized she was a student at the university and had been given this as an assignment.

Now the school psychologist is leaning toward me from across the table. She places her hand on my arm. She is wearing a red sweater beneath her white lab coat. She also is wearing a pearl necklace. I notice that her index and middle fingers are yellow. She is a heavy smoker. Her nails are short, as if she bites them. There are no rings on her fingers. Her sweater is tight, even though she must be over thirty. She licks her lips and begins to ask me in a low voice what I think of the school, what books I read and such. I know she is trying to coax me into telling her why I have said I can't run or play basketball. On the wall behind her hangs a picture, an autumn scene of a deciduous forest, with a girl on a horse, riding along a road in the foreground. It has a narrow gold frame. The door out to the hall is in back of me. To my left, stands a large, gray, metal locker. It is locked. The test results and files of all the students are kept in there. To the right, there are two grimy windows, without curtains. Outside is an empty lot. Beyond, there are rows of red brick tenement buildings. They were built before the turn of the century. This is a slum now. It is a cold, gray and cloudy afternoon. And, since I know what she is after, I talk about something else. But all the time I am talking, I look at her and smile. I tell her about the Bill books I have read. It takes her some time to figure out what I am talking about. I haven't used the correct word. I've said "lawless," instead of "outlaw." In any case, I don't believe she has read them. People don't read them in America, but I don't care. I'm only talking to set a wall of words between us.

She tries again. Her voice is growing very heated now. She leans forward and makes her voice soft. She wonders how I am enjoying my stay in America, and in this way tries to broach the subject of what took place in the gymnasium. She thinks I don't notice. I keep smiling and begin to talk about *The War of The Worlds*. I had heard it on the radio Sunday evening. First I listened to WEAB. Edgar Bergen had been on with his *sharp-tongued* puppet Charlie McCarthy. But I didn't find ventriloquism particularly amusing. I could speak with two voices myself. So I switched over to WABC. According to the paper, a play was scheduled. The *Mercury Theater of the Air* was going to present *The War of the Worlds* by Wells. I had read the book and wouldn't mind hearing it.

But the book had been altered to suit American radio. They pretended that this was a regular program. Some music came on, there was a news flash, then more music, more news flashes, and again music. Then they announced there had been an invasion from Mars, and so on. The book was much better, so I turned it off and went on reading *Quentin Durward* instead. I had been at it for several days. It was a good book, but rather difficult. There were many words that took me a long time to figure out.

The next day, the radio and newspapers reported that many people on the East Coast had become frightened when they tuned in Sunday evening to the middle of the play about the invasion from Mars. They really believed it was taking place. I tell her this now.

Finally, she interrupts me and says as if without ulterior motive:

"By the way, why didn't you want to play basketball?"

"I just didn't feel like it." I reply.

Then I go on talking about Louis XI and the hanged men. Sure the king was cruel, but he was doing it for France, something Durward understood in the end.

I could give her a straight answer, but I'm not about to. I don't run because I am not the fastest runner of all. I don't play basketball because I'm not the best player. And if I can't be best, I'd rather be nothing at all. But, of course, I don't tell her this. I would never dream of telling her, or anyone else. There's no need to tell everything. I am also fat. Perhaps Theobald is fatter, but then he isn't me. He gets everyone to laugh at him. He does it intentionally. I hate being fat, and when they laugh at me, I could murder them. But I don't tell her that.

Gunnar's assistant is married to a girl everyone says is very pretty. I don't like her. Although she is slender, she has big breasts and wide hips, which she dresses in tight-fitting garments. Her hair is long and black, and she has black eyes and a very big, very red, mouth. She laughs a lot. A clinking of jewelry accompanies her as she walks across the room in her high-heeled shoes. She also talks in a loud voice. Gunnar likes her. They came walking down the corridor. Gunnar, Alva, Gunnar's assistant, and the assistant's beautiful wife. They were going to the theater. They had a drink before leaving and now stopped in the doorway and looked at me, eating in the kitchen. They all stood there.

Karna had made little meatballs and mashed potatoes. She had prepared the meatballs with soda water, so they would be light, and she had added capers, because I like them. On my plate I put the mashed potatoes to one side and the crisp meatballs to the other.

"Do you see how he has already become American," says Gunnar. "He eats like some farmer form the Bible Belt. He sits ramrod straight in his chair, his left hand hidden beneath the table, and doesn't dare touch his knife, except to cut with."

"Didn't Veblen write an essay on the history of the knife in American eating?" asks the assistant.

"I don't recall if it was Veblen," replies Gunnar. "But it is an interesting subject. A person who happened to walk into an American restaurant without knowing the customs here, without knowing the social background of the Western European peasant immigrants in the 19th century or the cultural level and traditions of the Eastern European immigrants, might easily draw the conclusion that America lacked toilet paper and was inhabited by Hindus and Muslims, who wash their bottoms with their left hand, and therefore keep it concealed beneath the table." They all laughed there in the hall.

I acted as if they weren't there. I ate. I looked up from my plate and looked past them with a particularly blank expression. Then I looked at the calendar with its winter landscape of snowy fir, hanging in the wall to the left of the door. I rubbed my hand under my nose, as if it had suddenly begun to itch. I wrinkled my forehead, as though I had thought of something important. I turned to Karna and said:

"Do you think I could have a few more meatballs?"

She didn't look at them either. She acted was though we were alone. I was glad. Karna was always kind, even if she occasionally got annoyed with me.

"You can take the four that are left," she said, holding out the deep dish. "The rest of us have eaten."

"He is going to be good-looking, when he gets through puberty and loses the baby fat," said the assistant's wife.

"Could be," said Alva.

"Yes, many a girl is going to suffer over him, if those hormones just do their stuff," said the assistant's wife. "You can already see that."

My ears were ringing now, and I could feel every breath I took. I had to force myself to go on eating and not let on that I

had heard, with so much as a single feebly audible inhalation or
sudden movement. Gunnar stepped into the kitchen. He came
over to the table. He reached out his hand across the table to my
plate, and, with his thumb and index finger, he squeezed together
the two meatballs I had saved for last, and carried them up to his
mouth.

"You don't need them," he said. "You are fat enough already.
Besides, they're tasty."

Everyone in the hallway laughed.

"Have you rung for a cab, darling?" Alva asked.

"It's probably already here," Gunnar said, as he stood leaning
over the table, eating.

Gunnar walked back to the hall and I heard them all move
towards the front door, put on their coats and leave the apartment.
The high-heeled shoes tapped on the marble out there. Then the
door closed behind them and it was silent.

It was Alva who suggested the next day that I myself would
benefit by losing weight. That way no one would have to remind
me about eating too much or about taking a second portion. It
would be to my own advantage to eat less. That was why a problem now arose in the school cafeteria. We bought our lunch at
school. We took trays, took what we wanted, ordered a main
course, paid the cashier and carried the tray to the table where we
wished to sit. It was like a real restaurant. And the food was good.
We could get second helpings, if we wanted, without paying
extra. At a restaurant you couldn't. That was because the first portion the staff served was quite small; the school didn't want us to
throw food away or waste it.

I received an allowance. It included a fixed sum, as well as an
incentive bonus. I could chose to improve my finances by helping
set or clear the table, by drying the dishes, making my bed, reading fairy tales to my younger sisters, and other things. There was a
list on which the various chores were assigned points, and with

the help of this list, I myself could easily calculate the correct
number of points I had earned that week. If I then chose not to
touch some of this money, and decided to save it for some intel-
lectually worthwhile purchase (books or chemistry sets, or the
like), I could obtain matching funds. I only needed to save half
the sum and could receive the other half as a savings incentive.
This system had been initiated in Olovslund, but was now further
developed. It was based on an attempt to replace the traditional
carrot-and-stick approach with a self-regulating stimulus-response
system, whose aim was to gradually achieve a specific behavior.
An essential element of this was my freedom of action; I was to be
faced with various alternatives of unequal value. For example, I
was free not to make my bed, but this was at the price of lost
income. In everything I did in this family society, I had freedom of
choice. But this system didn't work all that well. For example, I
chose not to make my bed or clean up my room. This was unan-
ticipated. I claimed that the extra time I had for reading and other
activities was more valuable than the points I would have got for
cleaning and making my bed. Gunnar and I argued about this.
Although I tried to prevent it, he opened my door, stuck in his
head and said with disgust:

"It looks like a pigsty in here!"

But I maintained that my freedom of choice had to apply not
only when I chose to work for the money, but also when I chose
not to. On the other hand, I did choose to set the table, take off
and dry the dishes, and carry the food when they rang the bell at
the dinner table. But I did all this so I could be with Karna, whom
I like. I didn't tell them that. I let them go on thinking that I was
just making rational choices according to the allowance point-sys-
tem.

Even if Gunnar got angry, and Alva said I had to consider the
fact that the family was a social unit and that I couldn't just refuse
to clean my own room, since it disrupted the comfort of the family

society, I maintained that if I had a freedom of choice, then I had a freedom of choice, and that was that. I also knew that what really mattered to Alva was that the system be carried through in a consistent way. And for this reason, the system was retained in principle, even though my room was cleaned from time to time, when I was away and couldn't keep the door shut.

I had read about Mayer's rats and understood that Alva was worried I might meet the some fate if she were to alter the system on me. I took advantage of this. Mayer had received academic awards for his experiments with rats. He had taught them to jump down from a board onto a specially-marked disk. When they jumped on the right disk, it opened and behind it they found food that they liked. If they jumped on the wrong disk, they got a powerful electric shock instead, and they screamed. It didn't take long for them to learn the difference between right and wrong.

Once they had learned their lesson thoroughly, Mayer altered the system and changed the disks around. Proud of themselves, the rats jumped onto what they believed to be the food disk, and instead of the food they had expected as a reward, they received a strong electric shock that made all the hair on their bodies stand on end. They screamed. After this had happened a few times, the rats preferred not to jump at all. They just remained on the board. To force them to jump and choose a disk, Mayer aimed a strong draft of icy air at them with the aid of a fan. Now the rats jumped, and according to their previous training, they chose the disc they associated with food. Mayer again gave them powerful shocks. After that, most of the rats began to exhibit strange and neurotic behavior. They screamed if Mayer picked them up. They refused food. Some suffered cramps. There was one in particular that was interesting. It was she who won Mayer a great prize. She was evidently hereditarily predisposed to serious neurotic and hysteric states. Once she had been given an electric shock instead of food, she totally refused further participation in the experiment. She held convulsively to the board, even when Mayer placed the fan right on her. It was only after Mayer poured ice water on her drop by drop, that she screamed and jumped from the board with exaggerated vigor. This rat then had a fit, for when she was finally forced to jump, Mayer gave her repeated electric shocks. She ran around haphazardly, wild at the bottom of the cage, until she ended up on the floor in a total cataleptic state. For the rest of her life this rat became a loner; she isolated herself and became asocial. Each time Mayer forced this rat to make a choice, the hysterical behavior returned. She howled and screamed and ran around in a frenzy, finally falling into a cataleptic state again.

This rat became truly famous in the annals of psychological research. Many professors with their assistants and students came to observe her, as she ran around, screamed, and finally fell over. With this rat, Mayer was able to clinically prove and record the origin of neuroses, and to scientifically support the hypothesis that different individuals are unequally predisposed to neurotic and hysterical behavior. But if some of Mayer's rats went totally crazy, they all reacted with a certain amount of confusion and unease when faced with conflicting behavioral conditioning. I know that was why Alva didn't want to change her system. She was afraid she had conditioned me in a certain way with her points and that Gunnar would disrupt this by complaining about how my room looked. I was following the system, even though I wasn't doing it the way she had intended. I understood her reasoning and took advantage of it. I could do as I wished, because she thought the way she did. But Alva didn't even understand the rats.

Alva had told me once about Mayer and his rats. I pictured Mayer as a very tall, thin, man in a white coat and bow tie. He was totally bald and wore steel-rimmed glasses; his two upper front teeth stuck out and were gold capped. He proudly held out a dead rat toward his audience. He held her by the tail, and then the president of the Academy awarded him the Distinguished

Medal of Science.

Alva felt that Mayer had done something important. But that was because she didn't understand animals and couldn't handle them like normal people. Mayer, who tortured his rats until they screamed, was just a mad scientist, the kind you saw and read about in comic books. I knew how to treat rats. I used to have white mice. They were not too bright, but you could teach them a few things.

Folke and Stig, and everyone else who lived out in the country, knew something of animal behavior. They knew that animals could become unhappy and lose the will to live, or might scream and bite if they were mistreated, that different animals felt and thought differently, even though they might be of the same species, perhaps the same litter. This was known by everyone who had ever had anything to do with animals. They understood this without first having to torment and torture the creatures, like Mayer and other psychologists and scientists in their white coats. But I didn't bother telling Alva this. She just didn't understand animals.

Folke said that no matter how intelligent dogs were, you had to remember that they couldn't think for themselves the way we could. So that I wouldn't forget this, he told me the story of the men who lived in a small town in Germany with his fine pedigreed boxer, considered by all to be highly intelligent. Every evening when the German came home from work and sat smoking in his armchair, he would say:

"The paper!"

The dog would get up, walk to the door and open it by pushing the latch with his paw. He would go out and down the street, and across the next street to the newspaper stand, where he would get a newspaper and then return home to his master. The German was very proud of his dog.

Then, one day, the man moved to another city, in another part of Germany. That evening their new neighbors dropped in for a visit. They sat drinking beer and schnapps. The man bragged about his dog, telling them how intelligent it was. He wanted to show them and said:

"The paper!"

But the boxer just crawled to a corner and began to whine. The man grew angry. The dog was making a laughing stock out of him in front of the new neighbors, so he stamped his foot and shouted:

"The paper!"

At that, the boxer trudged to the door and slipped out. It was only a little later that the man remembered that, while he had walked past the new newspaper stand and told the dog that this was the place he would be getting the paper, he hadn't actually trained the dog to go and get the paper from that stand. He began to regret what he had done; his was a fine and valuable animal that had won many prizes and was sought after for breeding. He went out into the street. He called and looked for his dog, but it was gone.

One night, about two weeks later, the German heard a scratching at his door. There stood the dog with some tattered bits of newspaper in its mouth. The animal was emaciated and walked with a limp. It was in such bad shape that it couldn't be saved and had to be shot. It was the German's own fault.

The dog had been given an order. It had thought it madness, but was obedient and had done what it was told. There were dogs like that. Other dogs just refused to obey orders they considered foolish. There were still others which grew vicious and irritable, when given too many orders they did not understand. That's the way animals are. That's why not everyone makes a good pet owner or can get along with them. You have to be very careful what you say to an animal. And if you taught them something, you should not order them to do the opposite thing just like that.

There was a fellow in Strängnäs who thought it fun to play tricks on his dog. One day, he finally went too far. He had taught the dog to come and eat when he said, "Yummy,yummy!" One Saturday, when he was drunk, he held out a bone and called "Yummy, yummy!" and when the dog came, tail wagging happily, he gave him a hard slap on the nose and shouted, "Naughty!" He grinned at the dog when he hit him. At this, the dog bit him. This fellow from Strängnäs lost his ring finger and little finger, when his hand got infected it had to be operated on. The dog had to be shot, since it had caused injury.

"People like that shouldn't be allowed to keep pets!" Folke had said.

He felt that people should respect animals.

Sometime later, I sat with Träff in the kennel and told him about the dog that had been ordered to run almost the whole way across Germany. But Träff didn't look like he would bother obeying, if I were to give him an order like that. Träff thought of me more like a dog than a human being. Or only like a semi-human. One he didn't have to obey but could play with. But when Folke said something to him, it was different. If Folke had given him that kind of order, Träff would have gotten up, looked at him, sighed the way he did when he was sad, and then slowly plodded off, to return two weeks later, half-dead. Or he might not have come back at all. But Folke never did that kind of thing. He didn't even have to give an order. Träff understood what he wanted anyway.

"Dogs know by instinct," Folke had said.

But that was at Kvicksta. Here in New York, things were different. Because I was so fat, Alva had made the school lunch part of the system. I was given responsibility for my own lunch money. This way I would choose to get less food of my own free will, so I would have more money to buy books with. The lunch money that could be spent in the school cafeteria was added to my allowance and I was given a free choice. That's when the trouble started in the cafeteria. The first day no one said anything when I just took a glass of water and a piece of bread. They probably thought I wasn't feeling well. The next day I took an apple and they wondered. But the third day, when I just took a small portion of porridge, they began to speak to me. I explained to them that I couldn't afford to eat more. I was saving my money. They tried to make me change my mind and eat. They even said that I didn't have to pay so much, if I just ate. But I didn't eat. And I wasn't hungry. You don't have to eat.

It wasn't because of the money that I had stopped eating lunch. I had also stopped eating breakfast. It was because I was fat and hated being fat. I hated looking at myself in the mirror. I thought of Theobald when I saw myself in the mirror. It seemed to me that I sloshed around. I spit on my reflection when I was alone in the bathroom with the door locked. Then I wiped off the saliva, so that no one would know. I hadn't told anyone, and I wasn't about to tell the school psychologist now, either.

The school psychologist hadn't begun to talk about the cafeteria yet. I was pretty sure she would. I supposed it was when the the trouble started, when there was a problem both in the gym and at lunch, that they decided to send me to see her. I thought about what I was going to say. She would hardly believe that I wasn't hungry anymore. So I would just tell her I was saving my money for the biggest Meccano kit they made. She was undoubtedly familiar with it and knew it was so expensive that I wouldn't have to discuss how long I wouldn't be eating lunch.

But instead, she reaches out her hand and ruffles my hair. Then she strokes my cheek and throat, takes hold of my neck, shakes me a little and squeezes my muscles there. She reaches out her other hand and pokes her fingers into my back muscles. A hot feeling rushes over me. It is both pleasant and unpleasant at the same time. I feel the tiny hairs at the back of my neck stand on end. Each hair seems to tickle, and a heavy tingling sensation runs through my body. Her hands are very warm and seem to be crawling over me. Right then I raise my head and look into her eyes. I see her real eyes as she touches me. They are totally expressionless, as if they were dead. She looks past me, she's just pretending. I realize at once that she is only doing this with me because it's part of of her job. I had already known this. I should have remembered. In addition, she's doing it to improve her standing with her university professor, by showing that she is able to handle children like me through word and manipulation. I make myself stop feeling her hands, look out through the window, but continue smile at her as usual. Now I begin to suffer an unpleasant chill. I give myself a shake to get her hands off my body. She releases me.

She picks up the green file off her desk, instead. She places it in front of her, opens it and takes out some papers. I recognize them. I realize that she must have got them from Mr. Francis. The handwriting is bad. It is probably the worst handwriting in the class here. It was the worst in my Swedish class. Next grade, I can use a typewriter. Never never again in my whole life will I have to let anyone see my handwriting. She reads what I have written. It is, of course, misspelled. Everything I write without being able to use a dictionary to see how it is written, is spelled wrong. Almost every word. English is harder than Swedish. I knew I misspelled the words, when I wrote it. I knew this even while writing it. She puts the paper down. I have difficulty with the "k" and "s" sounds. When is the "k" sound spelled with a "k" and when with a "c," when is the letter "c" pronounced "s" and the letter "s" pronounced "s"? I lean across the desk and, glancing furtively, read. If there's one thing I can do better than anyone else, it is read my own handwriting. Mr. Francis thought this was a good joke. I had already tried it on Miss Rehn.

"I kant learn how to be systematic in my work." I read. It

should have been spelled with a "c." And with an apostrophe. "Can't and not "cant." I mean "cannot" and not "hypocrisy." I know the word, after all. Nor have I remembered to erase the comment I had made after trying to recall the spelling of the word "attention." I should have erased it. I usually do. It's the kind of thing I just whisper to the paper and then erase. It was unnecessary to let them see it. I finally wrote "etention," after having wrestled with the spelling a moment. Then I placed it in parentheses, because I was angry at myself and at my lousy handwriting. I wrote, *"I have none."*

It isn't really fault that the paper looks the way it does. There are people born without a little finger. I was born with bad handwriting and dyslexia. They've been testing me for it as long as I can remember. There is no relation between ability to spell and general intelligence, just as there is none between sense of color and intelligence. I know this because I have read it in a book. I've looked up everything they have said about me in their books and read about it. I have read about my handwriting and my word-blindness, and also about my being fat. I have read much more than they can imagine. But I write poorly anyway. I hate to reveal my handwriting and show how poorly I spell. The papers there in front of her should never have existed. I should have told Mr. Francis that day that my hand hurt or that I was sick, or I just should have told him I couldn't. The others almost never say no. They don't know how to make a person go away by looking at him, or to look at his forehead and say "no!" Or else they don't dare. But I can say no to anyone. I can say no to the entire world, if I choose.

Now the papers lie there in front of her. I have written on them, and in words they expose me, naked and fat. If I can use a typewriter and a dictionary, I write better than the others because I have a better vocabulary. I even know more English words than most of them. I just have to check on the way they are spelled. If

I could bring my typewriter and dictionary, Mr. Francis wouldn't have any problem either. The typewriter isn't half as noisy as they claim. Here at school, the older students are allowed to use a typewriter.

But I am also aware that it is neither my handwriting nor spelling that really concerns her. Like my weight, they are recorded in my file and she has known about them from the beginning. There is something else. They have discovered that I have been toying with time. I shifted a decade last week. It wasn't that I forgot to write the correct date when I turned in the paper. It was like when you stepped on all the cracks in the sidewalk. You couldn't suddenly change stride just because you got shoved. You had to keep going, or else start from the beginning again. I couldn't change dates and could only hope that no one would notice.

All last week I had lived in the year 1928. In Sweden there was a Jan Myrdal who was one year old, but I was here in New York. I had made the transition with the help of a perpetual calendar. 1928 was a leap year, like 1984 or 1792. The first day of the first month of the year was a Sunday. Then it was just a matter of using that time. For example, while those living in the year 1938 had listened to the War of the Worlds one Sunday evening, for us in 1928 it was a Thursday evening. The moon was also on a different schedule. So instead of writing "Thursday, November 3, 1938" on the paper I had handed in to Mr. Francis, I had written the correct date for me in my time: Saturday, November 3, 1928.

Actually, it was an experiment. If you wake up in the middle of the night and it's pitch dark in the room, how do you know what time you've woken up in? Maybe you didn't wake up at all, but are just dreaming that you woke up. How would you know? You could say that you know what happened the day before. But maybe you dreamed what you believed happened yesterday. You could say you remember the day before better than the dream.

But if you think about it carefully, you don't remember yesterday particularly well. You remember parts of it. Then you put the parts together. You create a yesterday this way. If I talk to Karna about things that happened yesterday, she remembers a different yesterday. Maybe we weren't in the same day yesterday? Maybe I'm remembering a dream.

I have just woken up and I tell myself it is 1938 out there. But what if it were really 1808, what would happen then? Most people would expect me to want to change the whole world. With all that I know from 1938, I could have quite an impact on 1808. Airplanes, cars, chemical weapons and radios. And all the gold to be found in Alaska and other places. But do I really know these things? I walk out into central New York in 1808, intending to build an airplane. But there are neither tools nor material. Perhaps I can manage to construct a glider. Can I even do that? How do I go about it? And though I've read about the Yukon, do I really know more about the gold there than all the others who want to go West in search of gold? And how can I get to the Yukon, which is Russian territory under Czarist rule?

What about the steam engine? I know a little about steam engines. And I know the history of the steam engine. There is at least one improvement I could make on it. But, now in 1808, Evans has been working the last six years in Philadelphia to construct a high-pressure engine, which wasn't to be achieved until toward the end of the century. (How could I know this?) If I were to speed up developments, I would have to come up with all the other lubricants, steam boilers and gaskets that must be invented and that thousands of people know must be invented and are working on. When you enter another time, you enter another world. You walk along Kungsgatan and then along Broadway. You must accept the time you find yourself in, as you are walking. And actually, I don't know, now in 1808, if my ideas on high-pressure steam engines and steam turbines aren't analogous to the ideas of rockets and space travel I remember from the time I lived in 1938, ideas perhaps remembered from my life in 2156, although at the time I believed I was just making them up. Even if you were to awake in another time, you couldn't change anything.

Everyone is dreaming all the time. They, too, perhaps are thrown continually from one time to another, from one world to another. Every day they make themselves believe that the particular time and world they are in are the real ones, and that everything else is just a dream. They keep the doors shut, so as not to know. They wake up—or dream—in one context, and believe they find themselves in another, believing that, too, to be the only real world. And then from there into a third. It is as if their real selves are no more than a series of blurred dream-images. They believe the correct time to be the time of whichever world they happen to wake up in. In other words, it is impossible to prove that you have not been in another world, from which you have awakened into this, or that you are not presently in the middle of a dream in another time. I have thought about this. If I wanted to discuss this with her or anyone else, I could say that I have climbed around in it. I have spent an entire week experimenting in various ways. You can do this with the help of a calender, or by closing your eyes and thinking and in your thoughts do as if you're doubling a pen between your fingers, or by lying perfectly still and slowing down your breathing, or in a number of other ways.

I say nothing of any of this to her. She wouldn't understand. Most people believe they exist in a single normal world the whole time. In fact, everyone I have tried to discuss this with has believed that you could only conceive of existing in one world and one time. They just became a little confused and uneasy when I asked them to explain why they don't think they fall out of one world into another each night. How can they be so sure they know when they are dreaming and when they aren't?

So last week I worked on moving to 1928, to see what would happen. It had not been my intention to really change times. You can't just up and do that. You can't decide a thing like that. If it happens, it's by mere chance. Before going to sleep at night, no one knows which time or world he will wake up in the next morning—if he wakes up at all. You could end up outside of time and space, beyond the universe or in a time beyond time. Before it even came into existence.

So my intention had only been to shift time around a little, like when you double a pen. If you close your eyes and cross your forefinger and middle finger, you can roll two pens between them; you can feel the two of them. But if you open your eyes, you are only rolling one; you can see it. Now, which of the pens are really pens? In the same way, I moved time around a bit by changing the calendar, as you might shift from a decimal system of counting over to a duodecimal or binary system, and get other relationships which also make sense.

But I said nothing of this. I kept smiling, and before she had a chance to say anything about the date on the paper, I said:

"I made a mistake there. It happens sometimes. It's like my handwriting and spelling. It's a kind of dyslexia."

I don't know if she believed me. But she couldn't read my mind, so it actually might have been a slip of the pen. She took a quick look at the papers. Then she put them down again and looked at me as I sat there across from her on the other side of the table. She had been feeling around in me now for over an hour, like when you stick a key into the hole in the back of a toy monkey, trying to get a grip on the spring, so you can wind it up and make it hop. But I had kept out of the way. After all, I knew her tricks. I wondered what she would try next. Perhaps she would take me out for a sandbox test. They would take me to a big sandbox, where I was to arrange houses, cars, fences and animals the way I wanted.

"Now, we want you to play just exactly the way you want," they would say. "Don't pay any attention to me. Don't let me disturb you. You can do whatever you want."

That way they could look inside you. I knew this, but they didn't know that I knew. It was a question of choosing the kind of world I wanted to let them see. I had seen pictures of how retarded children created their worlds through play, and how neurotic children created theirs. I knew what it meant if the child just tossed in the objects haphazardly, and what it meant if the child set up a great number of fences and squares. Domestic animals meant one thing, and cars another, not to mention lions and tigers. It was a matter of carefully selecting what you wanted to let them see. But she didn't take me to the sandbox-test room.

She now took other papers out of the green file and glanced at them. I couldn't see what she was reading. Perhaps she was going to try an association test. If she said "mother" I would say "father," and if she said "sister" I would reply "brother." She would start by explaining this to me. "Big" called for "small," and "here" "there", and on and on. And she would tell me to answer without delay, without taking the time to think about my answer. This was a more dangerous test than the sandbox exercise or the one with the colored lines. It was used to catch thieves and murderers. The test progressed and in the end the criminal sat there, completely unmasked. Alva had tried it on me, so I knew how it worked. She presented it as a fun new game. She had learned it at the university. First I read a passage about a burglar. He had stolen two large clocks and a pearl necklace. Then she had said it was a game where you tried not to give yourself away to the police interrogator. With that she began the association test. She recorded my answers. But she also observed and noted my reactions and behavior, and timed how long it took me to respond. She timed me with a standard stopwatch.

She had told me that his was an exceptionally fun and exciting game. It was a little like *Clue*, she said, or like *Monopoly*, which we had begun to play here in America. But I realized this was not simply a game, and that she was also delving around inside me. She wanted to open me and see how I looked inside. Everything could be recorded and used against me, used to open me up. It was not just the words I answered, but the loudness of my voice, the time it took me to respond, a brushing back of my hair with my hand, a kicking of my foot, or my sitting unusually still.

With this test, the criminal always reveals exactly those things he most hopes to conceal. If they could only manage to make the test really reliable. In America they did this with the help of a lie-detector test. The criminal's own body gave him away. He had no way of controlling the sweat of his palms, his pulse or consumption of oxygen. They could then remove the criminal's shirt, turn up his pants legs, bind him to a chair with broad, black leather thongs, and attach electrodes to him. These were cold and had been moistened with a salty solution to provide better conductivity. They could be attached to the arms and legs, and to the naked torso. The criminal held two metal balls, one in each hand. This way they could record his heartbeat and pulse and determine how his sweat glands reacted. They put a belt around his chest, which automatically recorded his breathing. All these instruments could be plugged into a recording apparatus and the test could begin. The criminal would answer the word "father" with "mother," and "sister" with "brother," and so on. The interrogator read word after word, and the criminal answered. And now there was no hope, for all the instruments ticked away, automatically registering the slightest change in heartbeat, breathing and the functioning of the sweat glands, while the interrogator timed the criminal's reactions with Hipp's chronoscope, capable of recording time intervals one thousandth of a second long. With the aid of the interrogator's many instruments, the criminal's every secret was mercilessly revealed. And the whole time, the interrogator sat in his white coat, the notebook and list of reaction-words by his side, observing.

What was revealed was what you were trying to hide. What you were afraid to say. What you wanted to keep to yourself. It was a way of getting inside a person, getting a hold of you and opening you up. I had given it a lot of thought and had figured out a way of dealing with it. The game Alva found so amusing consisted of me first reading a story and then pretending to keep it from my interrogator. But it came out in my answers and she hit upon it. This was a game they played among themselves at the university. They called it laboratory work. But it also meant that I, too, could manipulate the secrets. If they wanted to get at a world inside me, I could make up another world for them to discover, open up and expose. I could get them to do this by telling myself that I must keep this new world a secret. This way they still wouldn't be able to get at the real me.

I sat looking at her, waiting for their next move. I smiled the whole time. It was getting late in the afternoon now, and we had been at it a long time. If she would tried the association test on me, I knew what I was going to do. I had already begun. They grope. They have a key and try to open you. It is as if they are trying to open a can of sardines in the dark. They feel for the tab and when they find it they fit the key on it. As the key catches the tab it can be turned and nothing will prevent the can from opening up, and you can feel how it will be opened up inside you and however hard you hold it back, the top will be rolled off and there you are totally opened and naked. But if you hold back the tab and turn it inward, they never get a hold on it and then they can't open the can. As soon as the key catches and it slips into the groove, the key can be turned. Once that happens, there's nothing you can do to prevent it. The can opens smoothly, you can feel yourself being opened inside, and no matter how hard you resist,

the lid is rolled off, leaving you totally exposed and naked. But if
you hold back the tip of the can, if you hide it and they never get
a grip, they can never open it. They can only scrape at it. Still, it is
important to give them something their key can believe in. And so
if she gives me an association test, I must make up a secret she
can uncover, despite my resistance. What is more, it must be a
secret that will make me feel uneasy when it is exposed, otherwise, it will be too easy for her and I won't react the way I
should. If I were sitting strapped to an electric testing chair, with
all the instruments in place, my palms wouldn't have sweated the
way they had to sweat if they were going to believe that they
were really succeeding in opening me, so they would be satisfied
of my innocence and let me go.

   That is why I sat making up a story while I smiled and looked
at her. I had glued my lips together with saliva and allowed the
saliva to dry, so I would notice if I let a word slip, and I had shut
off behind my eyes, so that I would see what I was imagining
instead. My eyes were open and I half-looked at her so she
couldn't tell. I began to fantasize. I took Alice in the checked skirt
and had her run across a meadow. Her skirt billowed as she ran.
Then the great metallic monsters from Mars, with their claws,
came along on huge metal legs. The people in the city chased
Alice toward the monsters, so she would be sacrificed for the wel-
fare of the many. I pictured this image again and again, feeling my
heart beat. I saw her there, imagined her fear, and I knew that if
she gave me the test, it would pick this up.

   But she put the papers back in the green file, pushed it aside
and ruffled my hair once again. She said, "It was a real pleasure
getting to know you, John. We'll be seeing each other again real
soon."

   Then I was allowed to leave, and it was over for this time.

CHAPTER 15

A few days later a letter from school arrived home for Gunnar and Alva. The school wrote this sort of report letter whenever it felt there was cause to alert the parents. Mr. Francis gave it to me Friday afternoon, when I was about to go home. I was to deliver it to my parents. It was carefully sealed. It was cold and there was snow in the air as I walked down 125th Street towards Riverside Drive, the letter stuck in my arithmetic book. I had a feeling I knew what the letter was about. It was about me, that much was sure. As soon as I got home, I went into my room, carefully closing the door behind me. Then I began to open it. I always opened letters that concerned me. And I knew that this letter did. Whey else would the school write them?

I used a thin knitting needle, pushing it in high under the flap, where it wasn't glued. Then I began to pull up the flap. In detective stories and other books, they say you should steam open a letter, but that just showed the authors didn't know what they were talking about. If you steamed open a letter, it became wrinkled. A person had to be a blockhead not to notice it's been opened. But if you opened it by slowly and carefully rolling a knitting needle, you could get a the letter open so it wouldn't be noticed. Well, naturally, a microscopic examination would be able to detect it. It would show the tiny bits of paper that were torn away when the knitting needle was rolled and the glue loosened. These would reveal that the letter had been opened and resealed. Another thing was that I didn't use the same type of glue as the envelope manufacturer. I supposed they could see this with the help of ultraviolet light. But Alva and Gunnar wouldn't have thought of that. They were interested neither in microscopic analysis nor in what might be revealed with ultraviolet light. One

Sunday at lunch, I had tried to talk to them about how the French had microfilmed letters during the siege of Paris in 1870, about the delivery of mail by pigeon post, and about how they had projected the speck-sized pictures on a white wall and enlarged the text. I had also told them some easy ways of writing secret messages with invisible ink, but it was a waste of time. Alva's eyes were totally blank, and after a moment Gunnar had said:

"That's wonderful!"

They would never notice that the letter had been opened, if it were done properly. But the thing to remember about opening other people's mail was not just the careful opening and sealing of the letter. It was also essential that the letter be delivered the right way. You couldn't just come out of your room with the newly-sealed envelope in one hand, and say:

"Here's a letter for you."

This would immediately arouse suspicion. You were too eager. There was something different about your behavior; it wasn't the same as usual. Instead, it was important to act as you did while performing a magic trick. There, it wasn't simply a question of quick hands, but of doing something with the conjuring hand that you didn't even admit to yourself. Magic books foolishly advised that you attract the attention of the audience to something other that what you were actually doing. If you did that, the audience noticed what you were doing with the conjuring hand. Instead, they should have advised the would-be magician to act in a way that both he and is audience found normal and natural, while at the same time, with another part of his consciousness, directing the conjuring hand to perform the trick, without being aware of it himself. If they were to believe it, you had to believe it yourself. So I had to stick the letter back into the book, dress as I had been dressed when I left for school, and take the book. I had to remember the way I had come home, letting myself walk the entire distance in my mind, right up to the door. Then when I opened the door and came in, I had to let the Jan who had just stepped in merge into me, walk up to them as him, and say:

"Here is a letter I was given."

That would work, and no one would be any the wiser.

This particular letter, however, had been almost worse than I imagined. The school psychologist had written a long report on me. She had come to the conclusion that I was emotionally disturbed due a lack of essential close contact with my parents. I exhibited *"pronounced autistic traits"* and tried *"to avoid social intereaction (schizoid?)."* But a that same time, I was *"brilliant"* and *"superbly gifted."* although I was severely disturbed and emotionally immature for my age. And then there were the usual observations about my dyslexia. People like her never understood anything!

Since Alva was a colleague, she had included an evaluation of my test results. I saw that in the Rorschach test they had found color chock, as well as sexual chocks, and that I had tried hard to appear special. This, it seemed, might indicate an artistic bent. But she had also taken note of my talk of murderers and blood. Still, I had taken great care to avoid saying:

"This is a bat!"

while pointing to the claws; that's what the imbeciles did. I had tried to choose the right answer from the Rorschach book. I had taken it from Alva's bookshelf, read it and remembered it, although it said that only psychologists and physicians should read it. But that hadn't done any good, either. With them, nothing helped. Still, they hadn't been able to get inside me or to open me up!

After reading the letter, I was at least happy I had been able to hold my own against the school psychologist. I hadn't let her get inside me, even though she had tried with all her bag of tricks. I thought to myself, she was just able to peer inside through small, dark windows. You should never tell them anything. A single word to them is one word too many. *"Grin and bear it!"*

The school was now asking my parents to strive to achieve a closer relationship with me. Alva agreed with this letter. I heard her say so, as I listened in the hall, after handing it over. I hadn't shut the door completely; I had left it slightly ajar, so I could hear what they said. Now I pretended to be looking for something up in the cupboard. But I couldn't think of what I would tell them I was searching for, if they asked me. You should always have an explanation ready. But you could also just mumble something, make it sound as if you were saying words, but not let them really hear.

It was essential that parents have good relationships with their children. Alva agreed. They needed this contact for their development. She felt that she was doing all she could. She had already instituted "the family hour." Gunnar grunted some unintelligible answer. He rustled his newspaper to make her realize that the subject was closed. He didn't care for the family hour. It took an unnecessary amount of time from his work and study, and he had enough—yes, more than enough—work already, without the school writing letters to him about it; and besides, Jan certainly didn't give the impression of wanting to have contact with anyone. Actually, I agreed with him. I wanted to be left alone. His occasional scoldings and saying that my room looked like a pigsty and that I was lazy and fat didn't bother me that much, he maintained. That's just the way he was. But Alva twittered and replied that one had to take the time for the child's sake, that you had to make an effort. At least, she should. Then Karna came out of the kitchen and I pretended I had finished searching and went back into my room.

The family hour was the hour each day that Alva spent with the children. It was the hour before dinner. The governess turned my sisters over to her. Alva had allocated twenty minutes to each child. She played with Kaj for twenty minutes. Then she read

Sissela a fairy tale for twenty minutes, and finally there were the twenty minutes spent with me. But she had a hard time discussing steam engines and such, and I couldn't talk to her about the things I thought about, because she didn't understand. Once or twice I had tried to explain this business of dreams and reality, and time and all the different worlds, but this had just brought a worried look into her eyes. For this reason we didn't talk so much, but mainly worked puzzles during those twenty minutes. But I often claimed I had some important school work to do, and that way I got out of my part of the family hour. Gunnar always felt that time passed slowly that hour, and from time to time would call from far off at the other end of the apartment.

"But surely you're done with the children now, darling!"

And Alva would look up form the puzzle and call back.

"Just thirteen minutes longer, darling!"

However, this time, Alva must have clearly insisted that Gunnar pay attention to the school psychologist's letter. The following Saturday morning he told me that we two were going on an excursion. We were going to cross the river. He called down for the car, which was kept in a garage up on 122nd Street. It was a large Hudson with an electric steering-column gearshift and a collapsible dining table in the back seat. When the doorman called on the house phone to say the car had arrived, we took the elevator down. That day we drove across the George Washington Bridge, with a 50¢ toll, and then through Jersey City and Newark on Highway 22, and on to Somerville, where we visited Washington's winter headquarters, 1778-1779. This was a two-storey, whitewashed wooden building. Then we drove Highway 202 up to Morristown, where we visited the museum of Washington's winter headquarters, 1779-1780. There we ate pancakes in a diner that looked like a railroad car without wheels. It stood along the roadside and, according to Gunnar, had once actually been a railroad car. Then we drove in the direction of

Paterson. On the Super Highway, past Parsippany Lake, I got to drive the car a while myself. Gunnar just sat next to me and told me what to do. But then some policemen came along and got upset. Gunnar spoke to them and nothing happened. After we crossed the bridge again and arrived home, Gunnar left the car with the parking attendant while we walked up to Harlem to visit Father Divine's Kingdom on 125th Street. Father Divine was a black clergyman who had become God. When Gunnar told him that we were from Sweden, we were allowed to sit among the angels up on the stage and were given the best seats, since we had come such a long way. The entire congregation stood up and shouted *"Peace! Peace!"* to us. Father Divine preached and referred to us as witnesses, and the congregation rose to its feet again and shouted. And afterward, everyone wanted to shake my hand, for I was a witness from Scandinavia. When we got home it was late and Gunnar said that he wanted a dry martini.

"I've certainly earned it, haven't I, darling?"

On Tuesday the following week the school psychologist summoned me again. When I came into the room, I could see that she wanted to hear how things were going. I told her what we had done. When I told her that I had driven our big Hudson near Parsippany Lake and that I had been stopped by the police, she interrupted me.

"The police came?" she asked.

"Yes," I said. "They drove by and saw me at the wheel, and they pulled us over. They said they couldn't believe their eyes. Then my father got out of the car and spoke with them. He gave each of them some money. They thanked him and drove off. But I wasn't allowed to keep driving. You can always buy people like that, my father told me. It doesn't matter."

She just stared at me, and when I told her that we had sat up on the stage among the angels in the Kingdom of Father Divine, that I had met God himself, and had shaken hands with him, and when I told her that this God had praised us and that all the faithful had cheered us, standing there below, I could see that she thought I was making it all up. When she let me go, she didn't even bother to tousle my hair. I was never sent to her again. Now I only had to take the regular tests. As long as they didn't bother me about lunch or gym, things went fairly smoothly at school. It was as if they were getting used to me.

Just before Christmas, I am free from school and take the subway down to Macy's. I go up to the toy department, because there is a locomotive I want to look at. It's Lionel's new New York Central 4-6-4 Hudson, O gauge. It is very pretty. It is also quite large. Each and every rivet is there, and it is equipped with a real, fully-functioning Baker's slide steering. Naturally, there is no way I can afford it. It costs $75. And this isn't the sort of present I can ask for Christmas, either. But you can also buy the locomotive in several kits and put it together yourself. The first kit includes all the tools you need to build the model: two screwdrivers and two special wrenches. It also includes the frame, driving gear and cylinders, along with Baker's slide steering, and everything. That kit costs $12.50, which ought to be within my reach. Then there are four more kits. The whistle costs an extra $5.00, but it's just a toy, so I don't need it. The locomotive is so big and beautiful there in the display case that it hurts me to breathe when I look at it. And this, despite the fact that I have often told myself I don't care for this sort of passenger locomotive, but prefer a 2-8-2 Mikado, a heavier, less flashy freight locomotive, or a good old 2-6-0 Mogul from the 1890s, a train that has worked the branch lines for almost 50 years. But this Hudson is just so beautiful!

I don't go home after visiting Macy's. After all, it's Christmas, and I am off from school. Instead, I go up to the Hayden Planetarium, near the Museum of Natural History, at Central Park and 77th Street. I had been there before. It was not just a planetarium, it was an entire astronomical exhibition. At the planetarium in Stockholm there was just a permanent exhibition, and once you had seen it a couple of times, there was no need to return. That's why the place was almost always empty. But our planetarium here in America changed its program like a movie theater and it was always crowded. I had hoped they would be showing *The End of the World* but that exhibit wasn't scheduled until the following summer. In June 1939, the Hayden Planetarium would be showing the effects of a comet striking the planet earth, or what would happen if one day, in the distant future, the moon would come so close to the Earth that our force of gravity would cause it to explode. You could see those moon cliffs, as big as the earth's largest mountains, race towards our planet to crush us. Or you could see the destruction of the entire solar system by a wandering star, bigger than our own sun, as it enters our system, causing all life to perish. Now there was a Christmas exhibit instead. I paid 15¢ and learned that the star that appeared over Bethlehem had been a conjunction of Jupiter, Mars and Saturn; and that, too, was interesting.

I strolled about downtown all evening because they had gone out somewhere and I could come home when I felt like it. There was so much to see in the Christmas windows. In America, our window displays are more interesting and effective that those in Europe. Our windows are a show for the entire population. And it's not just that we want people to buy the merchandise, like in Europe, either. Above all, we want to show that everything about life is fun and joy. It was a little like Dickens, and not just a matter of money. The streets were full of Santas in long beards. They rang bells and urged people to come in and look around their elaborate toy displays and department stores. Walking around like this in New York was the best Christmas I ever had.

It was after this Christmas holiday that I began to think that people at school understood me. They let me alone. I didn't have to participate in their gymnastics, sports and games. I was allowed to do what I wanted, to sit in the library. It was a fine library. I was a member of the wall newspaper committee and took an active part in all the class discussions. Besides, I had to go almost only to the classes I wanted to, and could use most of my time to build models up in the workshop, or to study volcanoes for Miss Tyler, my science teacher.

She was rather short. She had a distinctive mouth, and straight, short, black hair, which always fell across her forehead when she got excited, and which she was always tossing back with a quick movement of her hand. She had large, slightly slanted eyes, and she smelled of soap, not perfume. She laughed often and talked to me about steam engines, earthquakes and volcanic eruptions. I liked her a lot and did the vast part of my school work for her. This was no wonder, since what interested me most in school was volcanoes. I wanted to learn everything there was to know about all the world's volcanoes on the large world map without names or borders which I had bought. It was a little more than four feet high and six feet long, and I had to lie on the floor when I unrolled it and worked to correctly locate the volcanoes and write in their names. I printed the names carefully so they were legible. I drew the volcanoes in red, and in this way the ring of fire around the Pacific Ocean was clearly visible.

In the spring I used a typewriter to write down everything I had learned about volcanoes, and I made the biggest science model ever built at that school. It was a five foot tall plaster of Paris model. It wasn't plaster of Paris in its entirety, however, because it would have been impossibly heavy. I had first built a frame of wood and wire net. It wasn't made to scale, that was too difficult, but my first intention was to build Mauna Loa on Hawaii. At the foot of the mountain I had placed small villages. Up above, in the craters, there was the eternal fire. To the side, next to the central crater, I had placed Kilauea, where the lava constantly boiled and glowed. Inside the craters, I had arranged small explosions and eruptions. I said it was necessary to build this model in order to see which way the lava flowed and how the villages below were destroyed by an eruption. Miss Tyler thought it good fun, and after I had worked on the volcano, it shot sparks all over the room. There was smoke everywhere and the whole place smelled of sulphur. She laughed.

I was busy constructing a bridge in the workshop. I had built bridges before, but only with a Meccano set. Now I wanted to build a typical iron bridge, a girder bridge. In real life they were riveted, but I was going to solder it, pretending that I was welding. My shop teacher suggested that I build it to a 1:48 scale, so that I could also use it for a 0 gauge model train. First I made a drawing. The bridge was to be a trapezoidal girder, for it was the framework that interested me, with the divergence of the various forces present in the construction of the bridge. I could have made the I-beams out of angle irons, but the teacher felt I should skip this work and buy them ready-made out of brass from a hobby shop down on 42nd Street called *Hobbycraft*. This wasn't cheating, my teacher assured me. If I had been the president of a railroad, having a real bridge built, I would also have bought pre-fabricated beams.

The bridge was to be three feet long and easily able to support my weight. But it was rather tricky and laborious, so from time to time I would take ten minutes to sit on the wooden bench against the wall toward the corridor and read *Model Craftsman*. By the bench in a pile there lay twenty or thirty issues, dating back several years. There were just so many, many things one could make.

I had made up my mind to pretend that the yellow brass was black. The bridge was finished one Thursday late in March. It must have been the 23rd, for when I return to my classroom, I am going to work on the wall-newpaper. I am putting up a clipping from the *New York Times* about Hitler's entry into Prague, when the Jewish boy with the large horn-rimmed glasses says "Yes, you were right. He took Prague, too."

We read the clipping. In the *New York Times* they write that this is the twilight of freedom in Europe. The newspaper can understand why Britain and France prefer to look the other way, while Hitler carries out the dismemberment of Czechoslovakia, since they feel they cannot do anything anyway.

"Yes," I say, "and you were right, too. They'll be starting a war over there in Europe any month now."

POSTSCRIPT

This is a representation of the reality of an eleven-year-old, as he changes worlds, almost 50 years ago. The horizon of the eleven-year-old is different than that of the ten-year-old. The perspectives have shifted. His way of experiencing has changed. Still, only fragments of the great events of this pre-war autumn 1938 and winter 1939 are, as yet, clearly comprehensible. This eleven-year-old horizon has determined both the style and the format of this book. It is not until the age of twelve or thirteen, sometime between the old Germanic and classical Roman majority, that it really becomes possible to see the world. That's another story.

The broad task I have set myself appears in the preface of *Childhood*. It should be obvious that I am not writing a police report. Besides, a police report written 45 years after events would hardly be worth very much. It is the eleven-year-old and his world that interests me.

When I published *Childhood*, an indignant denial was issued. Professor Myrdal's maid had not worn a waitress apron in 1934. If you read Alva Myrdal's biography, you will find that I attended a different school from the one attended by the protagonist of this book. In it, the two older children attend Horace Mann School on Broadway at 120th Street. But that information seems as strange as most of what Alva Myrdal tells about me.

That the two older children (in other words, I, who was eleven, going on twelve, and my sister Sissela, who wasn't four yet) attended the same school in the fall of 1938, seems totally preposterous to me. And I believe that what I remember is more plausible.

But, actually, it makes absolutely no difference. I am not writing a biography, I'm writing a story about an eleven-year-old who moves into a new world. It is in this context that the school interests me. Thus, the issue of the maid's apron is as unimportant to the value of the story as is the name of the school. What I am describing is an over-typical childhood, but it is no abstract childhood. I am describing a particular eleven-year-old. I maintain that I can write a more direct, and therefore a more honest account of childhood than many others, than most people, because I allowed the doors to remain open when I grew up. For this reason, the rooms are not shut. I can enter there and know what it looks like. I know people who lie themselves an appropriate childhood in interviews and articles. But maybe they are not lying; maybe they have forgiven and then invented a suitable childhood to remember and written it and got it printed. But as I have not forgiven, I have not forgotten.

It is not possible to write "in general." I am able to write this account because I have both been this eleven-year-old and could see with his eyes, and, at the same time, I am no longer this boy and am thus able to make use of him without the least consideration. He would obviously never have accepted my right to write about him today. If he had known that I would be writing about him 45 years later, he would have tried to shut me out. I know this, for he was I. But he is no longer alive. He no longer exists and has nothing to say about it. He is gone like the traffic on Broadway in September 1938, like the snow in Central Park in February 1939, like the evening conversation on the bridge last summer and the summer before. Only for me he is not dead.

To be sure, I have a personal motive for writing this work, one that is personal in nature, lacking in general interest, except as motivation for a book. I have already given an account. I am now 56, soon to be 57. It is important for me, before I am dead and gone, to understand how I became myself, to understand why I act and react the way I do. It is now also within my power to gain this knowledge. I have lived long enough so that I am no longer encumbered by too many illusions about my remaining prospects. Nor do I feel any special emotional inhibitions preventing me from going back through the doors which still stand open. All my relatives who were close and meant something to me then, are already dead. My paternal and maternal grandmothers and grandfather, Gustaf Carlman, Gösta Gestad, Folke Reimer, Stig Reimer—all of them dead now. Wife, children, and grandchildren, who mean something to me, and might, because of that, make things difficult to tell, have nothing to do with this time and these rooms. They aren't in them.

Alva and Gunnar Myrdal have announced that they have handed over all material concerning my childhood to the Labor Movement Archives, to show the world that I was a happy child in a good family. I haven't gone there to see the documents. Nor have I visited the archives in the United States. They don't interest me. The only thing I've done is point out for the Labor Movement Archives that according to an important test case heard by the Supreme Court, I as author have copyright, and thus, the right to publish my correspondence and other work, despite the fact that Alva and Gunnar Myrdal, through the Swedish News Agency, have announced that anyone wanting to read and publish Jan Myrdal's letters could only do so with their permission.

This attempt to erect and look after one's posthumous reputation is as foreign to my nature as rechiseling the family gravestones to make them politically unobjectionable. Still, I do find this behavior interesting. Outside royal lines, one finds it only in political families—soviet, welfare-state and Kennedy-liberal. It has not been my purpose in this story to give an account of how an establishment consolidates its position. This lies outside and beyond the horizon of the eleven-year-old. I do believe, however, that the story of this eleven-year-old can provide a key to understanding how the powers that be are formed, whether they are French-Radical, Kennedy-liberal or welfare-state.

There is a special difficulty with this kind of writing, however. It didn't surprise me that Alva and Gunnar Myrdal would contact a lawyer and set their political friends and relations in motion, when they heard that I had written *Childhood*. I am familiar with the reactions of political families, and also know how parties and organizations automatically react to safeguard the interests of their own. Why, once, long ago, the Social Democratic publishing house Tiden sent one of my manuscripts to the Swedish Government Offices for inspection; the text might harm the party. That's the way all political apparatuses work, whether Swedish, American or Russian. This doesn't even upset me.

What I wrote was no book of scandal. But it didn't matter whether it was nor not. Whatever its contents, Alva and Gunnar Myrdal would use their contacts to try to have it branded a book of libel before it was even published, and this way see to it that it remained unread. This was in their interest.

What I had written was not what they, with the help of a lawyer, claimed. It was a book about a boy's childhood, not a libelous book about them. But from their position, it was something even worse: a childhood they had not controlled, different from the childhood of the problem child Alva Myrdal had so interestingly described almost two decades earlier for the radicals and psychologists of the time in both Sweden and Denmark. I frustrated their attempts to stop the book by seeing to it that what I wrote was published in the newspapers and read on the radio to such a large audience that they wouldn't be able to put their mark on it.

But, of course, they did harm my work, and make things more difficult for me with their public threats and an appeal to the Press Ombudsman seeking censure against newspapers that had written about the book. The television station Sweden Two was so frightened by their political prestige that Alva and Gunnar Myrdal's lawyer was allowed to examine the literary program "Magasinet" made about me in 1982 before it was broadcast. However, there was nothing actionable in it, and I have heard it was good. I haven't seen it.

I make use of my personal experience in my work to arrive at a comprehensible recreation of a past time, a time that still determines who we are. But if I make use of the individual Jan Myrdal, this does not mean that I am writing about my private life. Not in any of these three volumes, *The Confessions of a Disloyal European, Childhood, Another World*, have I engaged in some sort of confession. This is narrative. I have been flabbergasted by the impertinence of certain members of the mass media. People I have never met, people who weren't even born in the 1930s, have shed tears in the press over how I have forgotten how I sat in my mother's lap learning to real. Others scold me for my behavior during recess at school, when I was nine. They indignantly reprimand me and lecture me in the papers, insisting that I must play the game by the rules and that I am being disloyal by throwing the ball to a friend and not to one of the players on my own team, and they don't even seem to realize that they are growing indignant over consciously formulated expressions on paper describing events which took place 50 years ago! There is no one—neither child nor adult—on that school yard they can force to see the light. They are grappling with shadows—perhaps their own.

What we have here are consciously written stories. To be sure, I attempt to write with a feeling of being there. The words should be direct. I wish to give the reader a glimpse into the rooms of the past. But I assume that the reader realizes that this is a created, recorded text. Jan Myrdal was Jan Myrdal, but Jan Myrdal is not Jan Myrdal. And yet the wheel keeps spinning.

◆ ◆ ◆

ABOUT THE AUTHOR

JAN MYRDAL is the author of more than sixty books—political and social commentary, literary and art criticism, history, novels, plays and poetry. He has also edited scholarly editions of Strindberg and Balzac, curated art exhibitions, made feature films and numerous television documentaries. Very few of these have appeared in English, and he is best known in the United States and England for his *Confessions of a Disloyal European* and *Report from a Chinese Village*.

Another World continues the story told in *Childhood,* the first of Myrdal's autobiographical novels about childhood. *Another World* won the Grand Prize for the Novel from Sweden's Literature Foundation. The third book in the series, *Twelve Going on Thirteen,* was awarded the Esselte Prize for Literature, with 100,000 copies distributed free to Sweden's middle school seniors.

Jan Myrdal was recently honored by the French Government as a Chevalier des arts et des lettres. He maintains his controversial presence on the Swedish cultural scene through frequent newspaper articles and appearances on radio and television.